On The Other Side Of The Storm

His Stormchasers
Book 5

By

Ronna M. Bacon

Isaiah 4:6 It will be a shelter and shade from the heat of the day, and a refuge and hiding place from the storm and rain.

Psalm 55:8 I would hurry to my place of shelter, far from the tempest and storm.

Table of Contents

Chapter 1

Shoving his sunglasses back on his face and pulling his woollen hat down further over his ears, Redmond Stuart shrugged his pack higher onto his back and then stood looking around the area. He had set out on his own, not even letting his family know where he was headed, having decided he needed some time alone. His family had been through so much in the last year or so and he had been there for each of his brothers and sisters. Today, he needed to get away. He needed time just for him, to recover, to get his head on straight again, he thought, to spend time with God. He was hurting and needed healing.

The light snow crunched under his feet as he moved forward, his eyes searching for what, he didn't quite know. All he knew was that he was tired and worn out and whatever emotion he could not name was hitting him full force. He stopped for a moment, reaching for his phone, searching his messages and then turning it off. He didn't want that distraction. He had come out on this trail, to this area, to get away. He had been told to hike the Bruce Trail, that ran through the province of Ontario, but he didn't want that.

He strode forward, his thoughts chaotic, not really watching where he was walking. He didn't see the men who followed him, had in fact been following him since he left his home. He stopped finally, setting his pack down, and reaching for the thermos of coffee he had tucked away, sitting on a fallen log, his eyes watchful, his heart hurting. He didn't know why, but he felt burned out. He had spoken with his father last night, asking for some time away. Riordan had hesitated but Redmond had just bluntly told him he was leaving on a vacation in the morning, that he had not had one in years. He hadn't waited for his father to response, simply ending the call.

He listened to the music of the wilderness, the wind, the birds, falling of snow from branches as the day warmed. He felt uneasy but couldn't say why. Lord, You've brought me here. I feel like I have been brought aside, for what reason I don't know. I just know I'm tired. I need to heal and I know I can't do that at home.

He tucked his thermos away and then rose, stretching, reaching for his pack, then stopping. His head turned, a frown appeared on his face and then he spun. Not quick enough to avoid the men charging at him. With a loud cry, he flew backwards, off the slight embankment, to land in a heap near the bottom of a small hill, rocks and branches falling with him, covering him partway. He didn't or couldn't move. The men watched and then walked away. They had done what they had been hired to do. Their task was to get rid of Redmond Stuart and as far as they were concerned, they had done just that.

Hours passed, Redmond not moving, the cold and damp seeping through his clothing. He groaned at one point as consciousness briefly fluttered in his body.

He didn't hear the footsteps that followed his tracks, or the whistle for a dog. He didn't see the figure pause before it reached for his pack and then stood staring around. The dog, a Border Collie, barked, before it scampered down to where Redmond lay, its paws trying to dig through the debris.

Sloane Everett, her own pack dropping to the ground, swiftly followed her dog, sliding down carefully to stop beside it, her eyes on the pile of debris before she gave an exclamation, her hands reaching for Redmond before she looked back up the hill. She gently touched her dog, a whisper spoken, and he was up and away from her. Sloane knew he would find her brother. She didn't know who had asked them to search for this man, but someone had. Someone had been concerned enough about his safety. She would ask when they got him out. She raced back up the hill for her pack and was down beside him in no time.

She gently moved the debris from him, sitting back on many occasions to watch him, assessing hm. She felt for a pulse, grateful he was still alive. She finally had enough of an area cleared she could do a better assessment.

Then, she paused, her head turning to listen. There were voices, men's voices, but she didn't recognize them. She prayed that they were hidden enough, that they would not be seen. She heard the anger in the voices, anger that drove fear through her.

She watched through the trees, trying to see enough of the men to get a description but they remained too far back from the edge. She sighed. Lord, I could use some help about now. I think I just got involved in something I don't want to be involved in. Why me, Lord? I don't like conflict. I try to avoid it, but it looks as if that very thing has come my way.

She jumped as she heard a scuffling beside her in the brush and spun, her hand to her chest.

"Shanley! You scared me." She glared at her brother, even as she wrapped her arms around her dog, Lad.

Shanley gave a quick grin, watching his sister closely. "Sorry. I didn't mean to. What do you have?"

"I have no idea. I haven't checked for any identification, but I think it might be the man we were sent out to find." She looked back up the hill. "There were some men up there a bit ago. I think they were looking for him."

"They were. Lad warned me they were heading my way and we hid." Shanley dropped to the other side of Redmond and did his own assessment. "We need to get him out of here. The thing is, I don't think we'll have time before the weather hits. Dad let me know there's a cold front moving in, expecting to bring sleet and snow. We need to find shelter." He looked up at the sky, feeling the sting of the sleet starting. "We have no choice, Sloane. We need to move him." He looked back down at his sister, a frown on his face for a moment, not quite sure of the look she had on her face.

Sloane stood, spinning in a circle before she stopped facing her brother. "There's that old shack down the slope a ways. I don't think it's that far. Can we move him there, without harming him?"

"We don't have a choice, I don't think. It doesn't look as if he broken anything, but I don't like that he's unconscious. We have no idea how long it's been."

Sloane shrugged, even as she positioned her own pack on her back and picked up the ones belonging to the two men. "We have to, Shanley. We can't leave him here."

"I know." Shanley pulled Redmond to his feet and then over his shoulders. "Lead the way, sis. Lad, watch."

At the command, Lad went into a protective stance, knowing that he was told to be alert. His hackles raised slightly and he gave a low growl.

"Move, Sloane. We need to get out of here."

She nodded, her feet leading her down the slope, slipping every once in a while, her head turned slightly so she could watch her brother. She paused, dropping a pack and holding up her hand.

"Sloane?" Shanley's voice was barely audible.

"They're at the shack, Shanley. Now what?" She looked around, despair taking over for a moment before she pointed. "There. The caves. They're not that well known. They're hidden enough we can start a small fire. The weather will help hide the smoke."

Shanley nodded, before he turned, slipping slightly, Sloane's hand coming out to rest again Redmond's shoulder before she

moved around her brother and headed for
the caves.

14

Quickly spreading out a sleeping bag, throwing it open, Sloane's hands reached to help her brother lower Redmond down to the ground, her hands around his neck and head. She tucked the sleeping bag around him, her eyes watchful, seeing Lad creeping close to the man, tight enough that his own body warmth would help to warm Redmond.

Shanley took a look at his sister, shook his head, and then hunted up enough fallen branches to start a small fire. He sank down beside Sloane, an arm around her even as he prayed for the man in front of them.

"Shanley? Is he going to be okay?"

Shanley just shook his head. "I don't know, Sloane. We'll have to wait until we can get him to help. And that doesn't look as if it will be a while." He turned to his pack, pulling out a thermos. "Here, Mom sent tea for you."

"I have some. You drink that." She looked down at Redmond, her hand going out to brush back the dark auburn hair. "Why?"

"Why what, Sloane?" Shanley had stood, heading for the entrance, intent on finding an evergreen and cutting off some boughs to make a seat for his sister.

"Why him? What did he do?"

"That we can ask him later." He turned, his eyes thoughtful as he studied his sister as she tightened the band holding back her dark blond hair. "I have no idea. Dad didn't either. It's strange how we were asked. It wasn't his family. I know that much."

Redmond finally stirred a few hours later, his dark brown eyes cracking up. He frowned, staring at the flickering shadows on the wall, before his head turned and he fought the nausea that very movement brought. He felt a gentle hand touch his face and then raise his head enough for him to swallow from the cup held to his lips. His eyes closed as he fought the headache and the nausea, almost losing the battle, trying hard to listen to the soft melodious voice that spoke to him.

Sloane sat back on her heels, her green eyes with the curious amber tint on Redmond before they raised to her brother. "Shanley? He's been awake, but I'm not sure how he is."

Shanley moved his sister to one side, taking her spot, assessing Redmond. "He's got a brutal headache, I'd say. We can't give him anything, though, not until we can get him somewhere to be imaged." Shanley was a physician working in the local hospital. He looked up at his sister. "God knew we were needed today, Sloane. I was asked to work this weekend but declined, having spent too many hours there already this week."

"I know.   I just wish this was different."   She rose, her arms wrapped around her abdomen as she paced to the entrance, staring out at the slick landscape now being covered with light snow. "How are we ever to get out of here?   It's so treacherous out there."

"I had enough bars to get a text message out to Dad and let him know where we are and that we have the man."

"Shanley, did we check for identification? How do we know this is the man we were sent to find?"

Shanley stared at his sister. "I thought you had." When she shook her head, he sighed. "Let me see if I can find a wallet." He pulled out Redmond's wallet, hesitated before he opened it, and carefully slid out the driver's license. He froze, shock on his face. "This isn't him, Sloane. We were to find an Eric Matthews. This says he's Redmond Stuart."

"Stuart?" Sloane sat back, shock on her face. "How? If he's not Matthews, then what was he doing out there? And what happened to him?"

Shanley stared down at Redmond, lost in thought. "I have no idea, Sloane." His arm around his sister, he felt her shaking. "Sloane?"

"Is he related to that message I took a while ago? It was to a Reilly Stuart." She stared at her brother before she scrubbed at her face, her hands shaking. "Shanley, Shamus sent me. He couldn't go himself. He was working undercover at the time." She mentioned their youngest brother. "He asked me to find the man and warn him about his youngest sister. I can't remember the message now. All I know is that I was scared, more scared than I had been ever before, when he asked me." She pointed at Redmond. "Now we have a Redmond Stuart? How is he related"

"A brother, I would think. I've seen them around town. If I remember, he's the oldest. Reilly is the youngest brother. Why did Shamus ask you to go see him again?"

"He was worried around Reilly and his girlfriend. He just asked if I could take a message for him. I didn't think twice. He hardly ever asks for a favour."

Shanley's attention was drawn back to Redmond as the other man became to move restlessly, soft moans coming from him. "I need to get him back, Sloane. I need to know what's going on with him."

"I know you do, Shanley. I just don't know how. It doesn't look as if it's going to stop snowing any time soon."

"I know, Sloane." He arose and hugged his sister. "Why don't you grab some sleep? I'm okay for a while."

She finally sighed, sinking down on her sleeping bag, her eyes on Redmond, before she prayed. She had no idea what they were facing but she just knew in her heart her life was now entwined with his and all she could feel was a great terror of the unknown.

Chapter 3

Stirring in the early morning hours, shivers running through him in a shuddering wave, Redmond's eyes fluttered open. He reached to rub at his face, frowning at the pain he felt as he moved. He sighed, wondering just what he had gone and done that he didn't remember going and doing, or which one of his brothers had tackled him hard in a game of football. His eyes fully open, his frown deepened as he took in the rock ceiling and then as he carefully turned his head, the rock walls, the small fire burning brightly near the entrance that was still dark. He could hear the crackle of the fire and the slight tinkle of sleet hitting outside and hissing at it blew towards the fire.

He sighed. He hurt. Hurt all over. And he had no idea why. His hand rested on the back of his head, finding the sorest spot and wincing. He flinched as he felt a hand gently grasp his hand and lower it back to his chest, tucking the sleeping bag around him once more. The same hand lifted his head, allowing him to sip from the mug before blackness once more claimed him.

Sloane set the mug down, reaching to tuck the sleeping bag tighter around Redmond, her hand resting for a moment on his face, her heart raising in prayer for healing for this man. Somehow she had been entwined in his life and she felt fear, a fear she had never felt before. She was known to be fearless when heading out on search and rescues, had been in some dangerous situations in world disaster areas, but never, she thought, had she felt the fear that drove so deep within her.

She moved to stretch out in her own sleeping bag, Lad tight to her, his chin on her arms, his brown eyes on Redmond. He wasn't quite sure of this new man his mistress was caring for but so far, he decided, he didn't appear ready to harm her. He would remain watchful, just in case.

Shanley had been laying still, his own eyes on his sister. There was something different about her in this early morning, something he couldn't quite place. He sighed. He had been praying for her more than he had been lately, feeling something building around her, what he wasn't quite sure. He just sensed danger approaching her and he wanted to keep that away, only it didn't look like he would be able to. He rose, shrugging into his heavy jacket, woollen hat and gloves, and stepping outside, his face turning up to the sky. It was beginning to lighten and the sleet and snow were easing off. He prayed they'd be able to leave at some point. He turned back slightly to stare towards the cave before he carefully moved around, heading towards the shack, stopping every once and a while to listen. He approached the shack, finding it empty. It looked as if the men had moved over the night before. He prayed they had made it out. They didn't need to run into any more danger than they already had from them. He searched the shack before pausing, a thoughtful look on his face. This would be a better place to wait, he thought. He reached for his phone, finding some service, and sent a quick text out to his father, receiving an instant reply. Good, he thought. Dad will move in as soon as he can.

He turned back towards the cave, hearing Lad barking wildly and in an angry manner. He picked up his pace, sliding to a halt just outside the entrance, hearing his sister cry out in pain. He edged forward, hearing for the first time other voices.

Sloane struggled to free her wrist from the hard grasp it was held in, tears sparkling in her eyes from the painful blow she had taken to her arm before the man had twisted it away from her. She prayed Shanley didn't return, not yet, or if he did, he stayed free and found them a way out. Her eyes dropped to Redmond, thankful that he wasn't moving or awake. At least she didn't think he was. His head tossed restlessly and she could see the faint redness on his cheeks, from a fever she suspected.

Her attention back on the men, she shook her head and pulled harder on her arm.

"I don't know who that is. I don't know that man. Who is he?" She bit back a cry. "I don't know Eric Matthews."

"You do. That's him." The leader of the men pointed at Redmond. "We know that's him."

"It's not. It's not him." Sobs finally broke through, tears sparkling on her cheeks. "It's not. Please, let us go. I need to tend to him. He's sick."

She was shoved violently to the other side of the cave, hitting the wall and crumpling down, a hand to her shoulder that had hit first. She lay still, her eyes on Redmond, before she crawled to him, an arm around him as she crouched beside him, Lad tight to her, lips back in a snarl, low growls sounding from him.

The three men in the cave huddled near the entrance, their eyes on the younger couple, even as arguments and angry words broke from them. The leader paced away, finally standing over top of Sloane, his eyes on her before he bent, pulling off her boots and tossing them to one of the men before he did the same to Redmond. He then angrily tugged her jacket from her and roughly pulled Redmond's from him. The packs and sleeping bags were gathered up and the fire extinguished before they walked away, taking everything the two needed to survive the cold.

Sloane angrily wiped at tears on her face as she sat upright, arms tight around Lad, who crowded close to her, his tongue out swiping at the tears. She blinked, trying to stem the flow of tears without success. Her heart raised in prayer, seeking comfort from God, trying to remember the words of comfort during times of sorrow and trouble and danger that she had memorized. She stared down at Redmond, knowing she needed somehow to keep him warm. Her hand went to his face. She had been right, he was starting to run a fever. She sighed. How were they to ever get him away? She jumped as she felt an arm come around her and then Shanley's voice as he prayed.

"Sloane? Are you okay?"

She shook her head. "No. I'm not, Shanley. Why?"

He sat beside her, his arm holding her to him, his chin on her hair. His sister was hurting and for once he couldn't fix it, couldn't make it better for her.

"I don't know. They were looking for the other man, weren't they?"

She nodded. "They were. They refused to believe me when I said this wasn't him." She stared down at her feet encased in the heavy socks she liked to wear. "How do we get out of here? They took our boots, our coats. Unless you can find them near here, I can't walk out. And they destroyed the fire."

"That at least I can fix." Shanley shrugged out of his jacket, wrapping it around his sister, who shook her head, taking the jacket instead and wrapping it around Redmond.

"He's starting to run a fever, Shanley."

Shanley stared down at the other man. "That's what I was afraid of. Dad's on his way. I'll let him know you need your other boots and a jacket."

"They meant us to die, Shanley." Shock still sat on her face. "They left us to die."

"I know, sis. I know." He stood, pausing in the entranceway to stare back at Sloane, who was staring down at Redmond before she moved enough to raise his head to her lap, her hand automatically smoothing back his hair. His brown eyes opened for a moment and he stared up at her, a frown on his face.

"I'm sorry? Do I know you?" His voice was hardly above a whisper, pain filled at that.

"No, you don't. I'm Sloane. We're trying to find a way to get you to safety."

He sighed, his hand reaching for hers, his grip strong even in his weakened state. "Don't leave me. I need you."

She sighed, watching as his eyes closed. She prayed her father reached them soon. She could feel the cold seeping in through her feet and watched as Shanley the fire closer to them before he sat, his hands raising her feet up to rest on his legs, his hands covering them as best he could.

"Shanley? Did you hear from Dad?"

"I did. He's about thirty minutes out. He has Shamus with him."

"Good. Now maybe we can get some answers."

Chapter 4

Four hours later, dressed in leggings and a heavy long hand-knit sweater, her feet encased in heavy socks, Sloane stood at the kitchen counter in her brother's house, her hands wrapped around a cup of hot chocolate, marshmallows floating on the top of the drink. She was still chilled, even though she had tried her best to get warm. She could heard her brother's voice as he headed her way, her father's voice answering. She knew her mother was around somewhere and that her other brother, Shamus, a private investigator, was off somewhere, deep in research. She sighed. Lord, what did I go and do? What have I gotten mixed up in? She set her mug down, the drink untouched, and headed up the back stairs to the bedroom level, knowing she needed to find Redmond and see that he had been taken care of. Something weighed heavy on her about him and she didn't know why nor did she like it.

She hesitated outside the open door to the bedroom they had carried Redmond too.

He had roused briefly, absolutely refusing to be taken to the hospital, trying to stand and leave before Shanley had agreed, stating that if he felt Redmond's condition was worsening, he would over-ride his statement and call an ambulance. Redmond had finally agreed, sinking gratefully down on the bed, letting the blankets be tucked around him. Shanley had finally taken his sister's arm and led her from the room, stating that she needed to look after herself. He watched with compassion as she had stood, wrapping her arms around herself, hesitation in her manner that was unusual for her, before she nodded abruptly and walked away, heading for the room she was using. Her own house had been damaged in a severe wind storm and she had chosen to stay with her brother rather than her parents.

She finally entered the room, standing for a moment staring around before she approached the bed, sinking down on the side of it, her hand reaching out to brush at the hair falling across Redmond's forehead before her hand rested briefly on it, finding the fever gone.

Redmond moved restlessly for a moment before he stilled, awareness once more rising within him. He felt warmed and cared for, and that surprised him.   He thought he was out on a hiking trail. With the weather he knew was moving in, he shouldn't be this content. His eyes opened and closed, as he blinked to clear his vision.

He looked around, a frown appearing. He didn't know this room, had never seen it before. His gaze stopped at it reached the young lady, sitting on the edge of the bed, her hand on his shoulder, her eyes closed. He wondered if she was praying.

He swallowed hard, before he spoke, his voice rough for a moment.

"Where am I?"

Sloane sighed. She had hoped to be in and out of the room before he awoke.

"You're at my brother's but you should be in the hospital. You were hurt, how bad, he can't tell."

Redmond stared at her, not quite sure if she was angry or not. He couldn't quite tell from her words.

"I'm sorry?   I'm not sure what happened or why I'm here."

"What happened is that my brother and I were out searching for someone, found you instead, and then had to spend the night in a cave because the men after you took over the shack we wanted to use. They found us in the morning."

Redmond stared at her for a moment, his eyes narrowing. "Did they hurt you?"

She sighed. "No, not really."

"They did. Where?"

"My wrist." She rubbed at it, her eyes on it, not him, jumping as his hand reached to stop her hand before he wrapped his around her hand and wrist. "It's okay."

"No, it's not okay. It's never okay when a lady is hurt. Especially if I'm the one to blame." He sighed, trying to shift himself up on the bed, managed to do so with her help, leaning back on the pillows she piled behind him. "Where am I again?"

"At my brother's, Shanley's place. He's a physician and has assessed you, but really wanted to take you to the hospital."

Redmond shook his head. "No, not that.   It would be too dangerous for everyone there."   He looked down at his hands for a moment. "I'm sorry. I don't think I introduced myself. I'm Redmond...". His voice died away, and he laid his head back. "Redmond Stuart. Why am I so hesitant to tell you that?"

"I have no idea. I'm Sloane Everett." She moved to rise, stopping as his hand rested on her arm. She tilted her head to watch him.

"The men? Did they say what they wanted?"

She nodded, her hair moving lightly with the movement. Redmond watched in fascination as the light played across it before he reached for a lock, letting it flow through his fingers. Sloane froze. She didn't let anyone that close to her, not even her family.

"Redmond? What are you asking?"

"The men? What did they want?"

"Not you." She snorted as he shook his head. "No, it wasn't you. It was someone else. I told you. We were looking for someone else when Lad found you."

"Lad?" At his name, the dog was up on the bed, creeping close to Redmond, chin resting on his leg. Startled for a moment, Redmond watched him closely before his hand rested on him.

"He found you. I wouldn't have. We think you were there for hours."

"And just exactly where? You're talking in riddles."

"In a heap of branches and debris." She was on her feet and out of the room before he could respond.

Shanley watched her walk away before he spoke. "Just a hint. Don't ever doubt what she says to you. She talks straight and true. A lot of people don't like that, but that's who she is." He watched the other man struggle to accept that.

"Look, I'm sorry. I didn't mean to offend her." Redmond shoved at the blankets. "Let me have my clothes and I'm out of here." He fell back, his head spinning at the effort.

"Not today, you're not. You need to sleep and recover. We'll talk more in a couple of days." Shanley had moved to stand beside the bed. "We need to call your family."

Redmond shook his head. "Not until I thoroughly understand what happened. But if I am bringing risk and danger to your sister, I'm leaving."

Chapter 5

Two days later, Redmond stood in Shanley's living room, a glimmer of a smile on his face that he was trying hard to hide. Sloane stood in front of him, hands on her hips, a frown on her face.

"You're hurt. You need to be resting."

"Relax, Sloane. Your brother told me I could be up and about." He walked over and sank down into a chair, trying not to let her know how shaky he still felt.

She shook her head, walking away. Redmond watched her, a grin coming out on his face before he reached for his phone. He hadn't checked it yet. Shanley had charged it for him, a question on his face when Redmond had refused to take it. He needed to check in with his family but he didn't want to. He didn't want to hear that his father needed him back to work, that there was another girl or lady that they needed to go in and find and bring out to safety. He had burnt out, dealing with his siblings' adventures as they called them. Almost losing his father to a gunshot was not part of the deal, he didn't want to be around his family if he was in trouble. Then he sighed. That was how Ryanne had reacted.

He turned on his phone, still hesitating. He scrolled through his text messages, smiling slightly at the number from his two sisters. The last one from Ryanne was so worried, he sobered. He sent off a quick message, letting her know he was okay but wasn't ready to come home, not just yet. He looked up, realizing he hadn't gotten that far from home after all. Just to the next town or village or whatever this place would be designated as.

He sat back, his eyes on an email from his father. Riordan was setting up a meeting for the family in a week. Would Redmond be there? If not, could they conference call instead? He had been thinking about the discussion Redmond and he had had about changing the direction of the family business and agreed. Now was the time, he thought.

Redmond's head dropped. Thank you, Lord, he thought. Dad was receptive after all. This will be so much better. We can train others to go in. That's a niche we can work in.

He looked up as he heard footsteps and a man appeared, one he didn't know. He took the mug of coffee he was offered, a questioning look on his face.

The man sat down opposite him, a smile on his face. "It's okay. I'm the other brother, Shamus. And you are Redmond Stuart."

"I am. Is there a problem?"

Shamus shrugged. "Not that I am aware of. I'm just not sure why they attacked you. You don't look anything like the man they're after."

"I guess that's good, but I don't understand this whole thing."

"None of us do, not at this point. Before you go any further, let me say I reached out to your father, not about you, but about this Eric guy, to see if he or any of your family know him. He didn't think so, but he would ask, he told me. That was this morning. Apparently, your family has scattered far and wide right now."

"They have? That's so unusual for them."

"Your father mentioned that. But he said with what Ryanne went through, it changed your family. They've all taken time to get away, to reassess what they want, and to spend time as couples. And he also said your new nephew was growing."

Redmond grinned at that. "He looks so much like Rory, it's spooky." He sobered. "But I don't get it. I know. I know. I've already said that."

Shamus shook his head, then turned it as he heard Sloane approaching. "Just a word of caution about Sloane. She's been hurt and hurt badly in the past. Don't hurt her, or you'll have us to deal with."

Redmond stared at him as Shamus held up three fingers and then grinned. "You sound like my brothers and my father. We always protected our sisters. That is, until Ryanne and then Shea told us we needed to back away and let her stand on her own two feet. He was so right."

Shamus laughed. "You can't say that about Sloane. She's always stood on her own two feet, much to our chagrin.

"Shamus, Shanley's looking for you. He said something about a meeting you two had to be at."

"And he's right. We do have to be at one. So does Dad." He hugged his sister before he walked away.

She stared after him before looking back at Redmond. She dropped to the couch beside him.

"Are you sure you should be up?"

"I am."   He reached for her hand, studying the neat nails and strength he could feel in it. "Talk to me again about what happened."

"I won't." She tugged at her hand and couldn't free it. "Redmond? Please? Let me have my hand." Her voice was barely above a whisper.

"Who hurt you that bad, Sloane? Who did that to you?" He watched her intently, no releasing her hand. "I'll let it slide for now, but I will want an answer."

She shook her head. "I haven't told anyone, not even my family." She blinked at the tears. "Why would you even care?"

"Because you are a beautiful, lovely, caring, compassionate lady, and I don't like the hurt I see underneath it all. You've hidden it from everyone, haven't you?"

She nodded. "I have. I haven't been able to talk about it. Shanley and Shamus would try to fix it and it can't be fixed."

"Sloane?" His voice was tender, startling her, causing her to search his face, seeing how he cared that she was hurt.

"Redmond? Why?"

"Why?"

"Yes. Why? Why would you want to know? You're a stranger."

"Because I care about my friends, and I would like to count you as a special friend. You saved me life after all, and I owe you that."

She finally nodded, settling back into the corner of the couch, tugging at her hand that he refused to let go. "All right. I guess I need to talk to someone. I talked to the

minister at the church when it happened and
he just shoved it aside, told me it was my
fault. Thankfully, he's not there now."

Chapter 6

Sloane shivered at the memories, reaching to wrap a blanket around herself. Redmond was watching and gave a low growl, reaching to pull her close to him and wrapped his arms tight around her. She struggled for a moment and then relaxed back against him, her head tucking up under his chin as the shudders grew in intensity before they subsided. His heart hurt for her and he prayed for peace and healing for her.

"I have to go back to when I was young, Redmond. Please, just let me tell me. I'll answer your questions when I'm done, if you have any."

"I'm sure I will. But first, let me pray for you."

She moved her head to watch him, finding his gaze on her. He bowed his head and she listened as he prayed, asking for the peace, reassurance, hope and strength that she would need in the coming days. She wondered at that, what coming days? What did he know or sense?

She snuggled back against him, not even aware that was what she was doing. Her mother had peeked in, startled to see that, and then moved on. She had to leave but didn't want to. She walked away, hearing the soft sounds of Sloane's voice. Lord, she prayed, let Redmond be the one who reaches her. I fear for her. Something is building for her and I don't think we can even stop it.

Sloane finally began to speak, the words drawn from deep within her heart where she had buried them.

She went back to when she was junior in high school. Life was good, she said. She was enjoying her classes, her involvement in sports, her church youth group. She was just starting with the search and rescue her father ran and enjoyed it. He had asked her to start training a new dog he had picked up, one he felt would be ideal for the work.

She had been happy, carefree, she said. She didn't have a large group of friends, but the ones she had were close to her and shared many of the same interests. She had no idea that an upcoming search would change her life.

They had received a call to go and search along an isolated trail one day in early summer just before her senior year of high school. They had gone willingly. She had the dog she had trained and was with Shamus. They searched along the trail, watching the dog closely, following as she headed away from the trail.

"This can't be right, Shamus. Why would she go this way?"

"She's following the tracks of the man, I suspect. Are you doubting her? Because if you are, it will affect how the two of you work together."

Sloane shook her head. "Not at all. I just don't see any trace of a trail. Do you?"

Shamus shook his head. "No, but she's picking up on something. Let's go." He shifted his pack higher on his shoulders and reached for his walking stick.

Sloane walked rapidly after her dog, her eyes watchful, still not confident they were heading in the right direction. She stopped suddenly as she saw the dog standing, her ears up, tail stiff.

"Lady? What is it?" Sloane froze as she saw the man stagger towards them, falling just short of where Lady stood.

"Lady? Down." Sloane moved towards the man, when Shamus' hand on her arm stopped her.

"Let me, Sloane. Let me go. I don't like this."

She waited, her hand on Lady's head, absentmindedly rubbing at her ears. "Shamus?"

"He's dead, Sloane." Shamus sighed even as he pulled out his phone. "I need to get to some higher ground but I don't like leaving you here."

"I have Lady. Go." She watched him nod and then move away.

"Lady, let's find somewhere to sit." She searched to find a spot under the nearby trees, dropping her back and pulling out water for both the dog and herself.

She watched the man, wondering who he was. Her hand froze on Lady's back as she heard a low growl come from her and then two men appear from the opposite direction they themselves had taken.

She listened to their conversation, fear rising in her as she realized they had killed the man. They had returned to ensure he was dead. She watched as the man was carried away, hearing the conversation more clearly. She froze, hearing names from prominent families in town, and realizing that she had just been witness to a probable murder and that she was the only one who could tell the authorities what she had seen. She buried her face into Lady's fur, her arms tight around her dog.

She couldn't tell anyone, she decided. But how did she explain how the body disappeared. She rose, her feet taking her back the way she had come, running towards where she knew Shamus would be, Lady following closely.

Shamus had turned as Sloane flung herself at him, his arms around her.

"Sloane? Sloane? What happened?" He couldn't free himself from her hug.

"They took him, Shamus."

"Who? Who took who?"

"The man we found. Two men took him. I was hidden so they didn't see me, but they took him away." Her words ended in a sob. "They left him over there."

Shamus' arms tightened around his sister even as he searched for an area to set her down. Finding now, he turned, walking towards the parking lot, knowing he needed to get her away from there and to safety. He tucked her into his truck, watching as the emergency vehicles raced up to slam to a stop near him.

He gave his statement, watching as the officers tried to get a statement from his sister, who simply refused to talk, just shaking her head.

He crouched down near where she had seated herself on the ground. "You need to tell him, love. You need to give them a description."

"I can't, Shamus. I just can't. Please? Take me home?"

He finally agreed, his decision not sitting well with the officers, but he promised he'd find out what he could.

Sloane never talked about that day to her family. She buried it deep inside her, not willing to put them in danger. She didn't know that years later, the event would come back to endanger her.

Chapter 7

Redmond hadn't stirred as she talked, listening carefully to what she wasn't saying. He had heard similar stories in the past but none affected him quite like this. Not even that last extraction his family had gone in on that had turned so tragic and that haunted them all.

He shifted slightly, still with her in his arms, feeling her body sag against him and realized she had dozed off, the emotions spending her strength. He sighed. So much for asking his questions. They would wait. Right now, this lady he thought of as a friend just needed some care and compassion. His sisters would tell him he didn't quite know how to treat a lady, that he wanted to solve all her problems. This time, Regan and Ryanne, you are so wrong. This time, God is showing me how to treat this special lady.

Shamus looked askance at Redmond as he returned, slipping into a chair in the room, Shanley heading for the kitchen, an eye on the clock.

"Redmond? Care to explain?"

Redmond gave a small shrug, an unreadable look on his face. "Your sister talked and that wore her out. She needed someone to hold her and I was available. Care to dispute that?"

Shamus shook his head before he stopped, surprise on his face. "She talked? About what happened in the past?"

"She did. I was surprised that she had but she told me what happened." He looked down at her. "She heard the men talking. They named people in your town as responsible for the murder. Did you even know that?"

Shamus sat back, stunned at the revelation, Shanley's words of shock echoing through the quiet room.

"She said that? She never hinted at that. Not in all these years." Shanley couldn't quite understand how this man, this stranger, had reached to his sister when none of them had been able to.

"Well, she did. And that has played on her mind since then. I've seen things like this. She say she talked to the minister at the time who shrugged it off."

"He would." Shamus had had no liking for the man and had been glad when he had moved on.

"So where do we go from here?"

"We? What do you mean "we"?" Shanley was challenging Redmond.

"There's a we. I don't walk away from ladies in distress, especially if they are friends."

The two brothers shared a look, even as they saw movement from Sloane, whose head was moving against Redmond's shoulder before it tilted as she looked up at him, a frown on her face. She sighed.

"I talked?"

"You did. You told me what happened. Now, we work to find the men responsible."

She shoved at him, not able to get him to release her. "Redmond?"

"Ssh, Sloane. It's okay. I've seen things like this before." He grinned down at her. "In fact, my two brothers and two sisters each just fought through a battle that almost killed each one of them and our father at one point."

"They did? I don't get it."

"You don't need to." His arms tightened on her. "I want to help. I imagine I have resources even Shamus doesn't have. I have friends in high places who will work tirelessly to find the men. And she's really really good."

She shifted again, seeing for the first time her brothers sitting in the room, their eyes on Redmond and herself.

"Redmond? Did they hear?"

"No. They didn't. You told me and then you slept. All I said was that you had talked about what happened and that you had heard the men talking."

She sighed, burying her head against him. "I didn't want anyone to know. They'll be hurt."

"They're already hurting, sweetheart. They're hurting because you are. The same for your parents. They're hurting too because you were hurt. To help heal you, you need to talk. If you won't talk to them, I can find someone you can talk to. In fact, I have a friend who runs a security company. He'd talk with you or his wife would." She looked up at him as his body began to shake with laughter.

"Redmond? What's so funny about this?"

"Because they all have been threatened, assaulted, kidnapped and lived to give God the glory that He spared them. I can guarantee you what you would tell them? It would not surprise them. But you would have to watch out for one of my friend's team members. He'd want to fly you away somewhere no one would ever find you."

"Where has he been? That's exactly what I want to do."

Shamus began to laugh, the sound echoing through the room, and encouraging Redmond in his search to help his lady.

"Not happening, sis. We'd just tag along with you. You don't get rid of us this easily." He settled back in his chair. "I know Shanley has food ready for us. How be we eat and then go from there on what we need to do."

Sloane glared at him. "That's what I mean, Redmond. He doesn't have enough excitement in his own life. Now he wants to take over mine."

Redmond tried to control his laughter, not being very successful. "It's okay, Sloane. He wants to help. At least you haven't said you were run over by a dinosaur."

She shoved away from him enough to stare at him. "A dinosaur? No one says that. It's always run over by a truck."

Redmond laughed even harder. "My youngest sister, Ryanne, did. She was adamant that's what happened to her. And in the process she laid claim to a friend of mine."

"She did what?" Shanley began to laugh, not quite sure what was happening.

"She did. She laid claim to Shea, said he made her feel safe. They are now happily married."

Chapter 8

Slowly pocketing his phone, Redmond stood for a moment, staring out the front window of Shanley's house. He should be heading back to either his own place or out on the trail he had started on a week ago. Had it been a week already? Lord, this lady is hurting. Help me to help her. She's opening up to me in a way her family says she doesn't do. Not to anyone. Not to her own family.

He felt a hand on his shoulder and looked to the side. Shanley stood there, his hand gripping Redmond tight before it dropped.

"When you do head home?"

Redmond shrugged. "I have no time line. I told Dad I needed a month and he agreed with me. There's a family meeting tomorrow I can get in on by conference call."

"Why don't you head for it tomorrow? Take Sloane with you. She needs to get away. It would do her good to meet your family, particularly your sisters."

"I thought about that." Redmond turned to face the room, arms folding across his chest.

"Ask her. I would suspect she'll say yes. For you, she'll go." Shanley walked away with that.

Sloane stamped the snow of her boots before she opened the door to the mudroom, slipping them off and hanging her jacket up on a hook, laughing at Lad as he shook off snow and then raced to find Redmond. He had claimed Redmond and could be found wherever the man was.

She appeared in the doorway of the living room to find Redmond seated on the floor, Lad on his knee, the man fending off the dog's tongue. She laughed, the man's eyes finding her. Lord, she is so beautiful, inside and out. Let us solve whatever this is. Protect her.

He rose, coming towards her, Lad as tight to him as he cold get, his hands reaching for hers. He stood, studying her.

"Listen, Dad would really like me to come to that meeting tomorrow. I'll go in person if you'll come with me."

She started to shake her head and then stopped, tilting it to study him, seeing his sincerity and then something else lurking in his eyes. "All right. I would like to meet your family. I want to talk to the one who said she was run over by a dinosaur."

Redmond shouted with laughter at that. "She really did say that. I'll even show you the dinosaur statue in the park that played a part in her adventure."

"Is that what it was? An adventure?"

"That's what we claim. She says it wasn't, that it was a life-altering event."

"And it would have been. Okay. So we're going. What time?"

"The meeting's for 10 a.m. If we leave here about 9 a.m., it's only thirty minutes to there. Dad's called the meeting at their home. You'll like it." He swung an arm around her shoulder, dropping a kiss on her temple, causing her to stop suddenly before the pressure of his arm drew her forward once more.

"Their home? I thought it would be at their office."

"Dad wants it private. If it's at the office, he'll be interrupted too much. That's what happens. And my friend and his wife will be there. You can talk to them if you want." He laid a finger on her mouth as she opened it to protest. "Only and I repeat only if you want to do that. No one has the right to make that decision for you." He sighed. "I sound like Shea."

"Who? And why?"

"Shea. He's a good friend of mine and Ryanne's husband.   Before they were married, he told me we had been making decision for Ryanne that we shouldn't be. That she needed to stand on her own two feet and make them herself.   He was so right. It was tough to step back and let her, especially for Dad."

"Yeah, well, fathers don't like that. They want to wrap their daughters in cotton and stick them away somewhere they'll never get hurt."   She knew her father was standing near her, and heard his laughter.

"As if I have a chance to do that, love." He hugged her, watching Redmond as he did so, before he nodded. Yes, Lord, I think he's the one. He has already reached down into her heart and brought out things we could never do, things and thoughts and events we never knew about.

Sloane poked at her father's chest. "You try, Dad. You still try. It's all your fault." She slipped away to head for the kitchen where she could hear her mother's voice.

"My fault?" William's voice raised in pretended protest.

"It is. You raised me to be an independent woman. Now you have to live with that." They could hear the smirk in her voice even as her mother's voice could be heard in protest as well.

"She's got us there, Anna. We did just that. With all three of them. And proud of them we are." He turned to Redmond, his voice dropping. "Can we talk?"

Redmond shrugged. "I guess."

He followed William to the library, sinking down into a chair, grateful for that as he was still tired from his ordeal and battling headaches on a daily basis.

"There's nothing wrong, Redmond. I just wanted to thank you."

"Thank me? For what?"

William sighed, not quite sure how to express himself. He was a man of few words, and when he spoke, his words were well chosen and well thought out. "Sloane. She's changing. We can all see a freer spirit in her than we have seen in years. You're reached her. Thank you."

Redmond shrugged. "It's what I do, I guess. Going in to situations and bringing out the ladies and girls we've done over the years teaches you to find a common ground quickly with them and to be ready to listen."

William was shaking his head, a slight smile on his face, wistfulness around his eyes. "No, it's more than that. God used you. We have tried. Her friends have tried. Her extended family. She would just smile, say everything was fine, and walk away." He paused to gather his emotions. "You didn't let her walk away from you.

Somehow, God used you to stop her. Now she can heal.”

“Did Shamus tell you what she said?” Redmond kept his voice low.

“He did. He says he’s working on that but getting nowhere.”

Redmond nodded. “That’s about what I thought. I took the liberty of passing on limited information to a friend, who researches stuff like this. She’s working on it.”

“Thank you, Redmond. Tell your friend I want to pay for her time.” He paused as Redmond simply grinned and shook his head. “What?”

“She never charges a friend for what she does. That’s a given.”

William stared at him before he rose to answer a call from Shanley.

Chapter 9

Her hand clinging tight to Redmond's, Sloane pulled him to a stop the next morning, her eyes huge as she stared at his parents' house.

"This is where you grew up?"

"It is.   It was an inheritance Dad received when we were really young.   It's been home to the Stuarts for years."   He tugged her with him.   "They won't bite you. In fact, you'll be running and hiding from all their thanks."

"Thanks for what?"

"For saving my hide.   That's what." He paused, his hand on the front door handle.   "If at any time, you get uncomfortable or feel you need to leave, find me.   I don't care if you interrupt my meeting.   You need me, you find me.   My family will understand."

"I can't do that."   She shook her head, stress showing on it.

Redmond turned her back to face his car, hearing the door open behind him. "Let me repeat myself and make myself clear. You are my first priority. If you need me, I want you to find me. If you don't, someone else will. I would rather it be you. And if you need to leave, we will. If you can't agree to that, we leave now." He watched her struggle before she nodded. "Please, Sloane. Don't let me force you to make this decision. I want you to make it. I will support you in whatever decision you make. That's a given."

She finally nodded, turning back to the door, stopping abruptly as she saw Naomi standing there, a smile of welcome on her face.

"You must be Sloane. Welcome to our home." Naomi reached to hug the younger woman before she turned to Redmond. "Redmond?"

"I'm fine, Mom. I had excellent care. Shanley is a physician, so there were no worries." He hugged his mother, holding on for a bit longer, knowing somehow that he was at a crossroads in his walk with his mother, that things would be different from then on.

Naomi stepped back and through the door. "When you two are ready to come in, I have breakfast ready.   The others are eating. No rush."

Sloane stared at her and then at Redmond. "Breakfast is ready but there's no rush? Mom would never do that."

He shrugged even as he hung their jackets on a hall rack and set their boots on a tray. "It's how Mom is. We don't often get to settle to a meal on time, so she's learned to be flexible. She says it's not a set time or a set meal that makes her happy. It's having her family around her.   And she has just welcomed you to the family."

"She did what?   Redmond!"   Her voice rose to a wail even as she heard light footsteps heading their way.

"You're part of our family now." He swung an arm around her as he turned to face Regan, who stood, coffee cup in hand, a smile on her face.

"Redmond! Lovely! Dad wasn't sure you'd be here in person or not."

"Of course I'm here. Sloane, this is Regan. Regan, Sloane Everett."

Regan reached to hug Sloane. "Welcome, Sloane. I've waited for what seems like forever to meet you." With those words, she turned and walked away.

Sloane finally remember to close her mouth, before she spun on Redmond, catching the grin he was trying to hide. "Redmond? Just what did she mean?"

"I have no idea. You'll have to ask her that."

"And I will." Sloane was away from him, almost running after Regan, who had stopped just inside the living room door, a grin on her face, another mug of coffee in her hand.

"Here.   You do drink coffee, don't you?"

Sloane stopped, surprise on her face. "I do. How did you know?"

Regan shrugged. "I took a guess. And I'm guessing you're after me to find out what I meant?"

Sloane nodded as she walked with Regan towards the kitchen. "I am. What did you mean?"

"This. We have never seen Redmond pay attention to any lady. Never. He's never dated. I mean, he takes care of us. He took care of the ladies we brought home. But he has never found the one for him. I think you're her."

Sloane sipped at her mug of coffee, a thoughtful look on her face. "He does treat me differently, does he?" She took a look at him where he stood, shoulder to shoulder with his two brothers, laughing at something Ryanne was saying to him. "They look alike, don't they?"

"They do. And they are gentlemen and Godly men first and foremost."

Sloane nodded. "I know that from Redmond. Do you know he threatened to leave, to not stay if I couldn't?"

Regan nodded. "That's Redmond. You're the most important person to him right here and now. You are more important that us." She held up a hand as Sloane went to protest. "Don't. Don't belittle his feelings for you, and I can tell he has them, or belittle your feelings for him. It's all so new for you two. Delaney and I? That's my husband at the sink. We dated during college but when Dad asked me to help bring someone home, we had words and walked away from one another. We lost years we should have had together just because we didn't talk through what we should have. And when we did meet again? We married quickly without telling our families and then a week later I disappeared and he was hurt. Someday I'll tell you the whole story." She paused, biting at her lip, before she spoke again. "What I'm saying, I guess, is that you need to bathe your relationship with Redmond in prayer, wait for God's leading. Don't be afraid to take a step forward, with Redmond at your side. He will support you in whatever decision you make, unless and only unless it puts you in grave danger. He would step in at that point if he needed to."

Sloane paused, her eyes on Redmond as his head turned and a smile crossed his face before he excused himself and came towards her, his hands resting on her arms.

"You're okay?"

"I am. Now, your mother mentioned breakfast. You made me leave before I ate." She brushed by him, walking towards Naomi, who stood waiting for her, an arm going around her as she introduced Sloane to the rest of the family.

Redmond stood, stunned, staring after her even as he heard Regan laughing.

"You just got told, big brother. And it looks good on you."

Chapter 10

Two days later, Sloane slammed the front door, anger sparking from her, bringing Shanley to the living room door.

"That's not how you treat the door, Sloane."

"I know. I'm sorry. I just had to have all the tires replaced on my car."

"What?" Shanley was at her side and could hear Redmond heading their way.

"They were slashed. Why? Who did I offend that badly?"

Redmond's face grew stern as he approached. Sloane rushed past her brother to throw herself into his arms. His tightened on her as he stared down at the blond head pressed tight to him before he looked up at Shanley.

"They know, Shanley. They know she found me. Or else they know she was there years ago."

"I don't see how they would know that."

"Sloane, think back. Did they see you?"

She finally nodded. "I think so. Lady made a noise and one of them walked my way. I didn't think he had seen us but he must have." He felt the sobs shaking her body. "Redmond, take me away. Find me somewhere safe. Please?"

His voice tender despite the stern look on his face, he agreed. "Go. Pack some things. I'll find a place for us." He watched as she ran for the stairs, sliding once almost to her knees in her haste.

"Redmond?" Shanley's voice caught his attention and his head swung around.

"Shanley? She can't stay here. That's a given. This will only escalate. She won't want you in danger. And frankly, I doubt you could fight them off." Redmond held up a hand as Shanley protested. "I know you would do your best, but this is what I do. Keep people safe. I promise. My life will be worthless if anything happens to her."

Shanley went to speak, but instead nodding, knowing Redmond was correct. "Shamus will have something to say about this."

"He can say whatever he wants. He can't dedicate his time to keeping her safe. I can. My family can. I have friends who will step in. She will be our main focus for now. Trust me on that."

"I do." Shanley's hand went out for Redmond to shake. "Thank you, Redmond. She trusts you in a way she doesn't even trust her own family." He looked back at the stairs. "She's never said anything, but she's had letters over the years, letters that scared her. She refused to show them to me. I'm the only one who knows. Please? Solve this? I like who she's becoming again. You've done that. Welcome to the family." Shanley walked away, leaving Redmond staring after him, his mouth open, before he ran for the stairs himself, to the room he had been using, swiftly packing what little he had.

He looked around, knowing he would not be back there, at least not for a while. He turned, hearing a soft sob from the hallway and approached Sloane, his bag dropping as he swept her into his arms.

"Sloane? Are you sure you want to do this? I can find some other way if we have to."

"I don't want you hurt." Her arms clung to him. "And you will be." She leaned back. "I didn't tell Shanley. There was a threat on the car."

"And did you give it to the police when you made the report?"

"I did. I kept a picture of it. They know you're here. They threatened you."

"It's okay, sweetheart. It's not the first time." He just stood, holding her as she sobbed, neither one of them seeing Shanley and Shamus standing there, anger on their faces before they shared a look and walked back down the stairs, deep in conversation, trying to think of a way to help.

"Mom and Dad won't understand." Sloane finally stepped back, taking the handkerchief he handed her.

"We'll stop and talk to them, if you want."

"No.   Let's just go.   Shanley or Shamus will tel them.   I can always call them."

Redmond gathered up their bags and followed her down the stairs, opening the door and then tucking the bags into the trunk of his car, shutting the door behind her. He stood, his eyes on her before he turned to Shamus and Shanley, standing nearby. He walked over to them.

"Redmond?"   Shamus's voice held concern.

"I don't know, Shamus. I don't know. She found a letter as well today. She didn't tell you that."

"Who was threatened?"

"I was and I don't know why. That becomes a priority with my family. We'll find out. I'll call in whoever I need to just to do that."

"I'll work on it as well but I have cases that I need to be working on."

Shanley shook his head. "I can patch you up but I'm not good at solving mysteries."

"Let's hope you don't have to do just that, Shanley." Redmond reached into his pocket, pulling out two envelopes. "These are for you. I gave your parents one earlier. Only open then if you receive word to. It has information in it I pray we never have to use."

The two brothers stared down at the white envelopes before Shanley spoke, his voice choking with emotion.

"Redmond. I know you will do all you can to keep her safe. You have our blessing if it becomes necessary for you two to marry."

Redmond paused, his eyes on Shanley. "Thank you. You don't know me well enough to say that, I don't think."

Shamus shook his head. "No, we do. We know you. And as you likely guessed, I checked into your family. You do have our blessing." He nodded towards Sloane. "Take care of her." He turned and walked away, not sure when he would see Sloane again.

Redmond stared at Shanley for a moment before he nodded and walked away, sliding into the car, his hand reaching for Sloane's as his head bowed. Only God could protect right now, he thought.

Sloane stared out the window, not quite sure where they were heading, but trusting Redmond in a way she had not trusted in years. And just why that was, she couldn't say.

"What did they say?"

"Who?"

"My brothers." She finally turned and watched him, liking the man she saw.

"To keep you safe." He pulled to the side of the road, shoved the car into park, and then turned to her, his hands reaching for hers. "They said something I had thought about but was hesitant to mention to you."

"And that would be?" Sloane watched, finally sighing. "You're not going to say? Let me guess. They told you to marry me."

Redmond shook his head even as a quick grin flashed across his face. "They did, and only if it was to keep you safe. The thing of it is, Sloane, I can see that. I can see us married."

She nodded. "I know. Now, where are we heading?" She pulled her hands back, tucking them into her pockets and turned once more for the window, leaving Redmond staring at her for a moment before he pulled away from the side of the road, not seeing the car that was following them.

Chapter 11

A week later, Naomi was on a hunt, trying to find Sloane, finally tracking her down in the office. Sloane sat at a computer, concentrating on the work she was doing online before she looked up, a smile on her face for the older woman.

"You were looking for me?"

"I was. Can you leave your work for a bit?" She seemed hesitant to ask. "Your Mom's here. We need to talk to you."

"Both mothers. That's ominous."

Naomi laughed even as she reached to hug the younger woman. Sloane had wriggled her way into Naomi's heart and family and the older woman prayed that Sloane would see that Redmond loved her. He hadn't said anything, but Naomi knew how to read her oldest son.

Sloane hugged her mother and then stood, back to the counter, her eyes flicking between the two mothers.

"Mom, what was it you wanted?"

"This is hard, Sloane. I just don't know where to start."

"At the beginning is what you tell me is usually the best place."

"Sloane, I have been where your mother is right now with you. With both my girls. It's scary, very scary. With Regan, she just disappeared and when she did come back, she was already married, had been married before she disappeared. You notice how low her voice is? That was from damage done to her when she was assaulted and left for dead at the end of her kidnapping. Ryanne on the other hand tried to walk away from us, to keep us safe by doing that. That didn't happen. Now, your mother is worried. She will be no matter how safe you are."

"I know that. I just don't see where you're going with this." Sloane heard her mother's indrawn breath. "It's okay, Mom. Naomi has told me to talk to her like I do to you."

"That's right, Anna. And she has been. With this, Sloane? There is so much unknown. I understand you have been frightened for years because of what you saw and heard. I understand that. But right now, what can we do to help you?"

She shrugged. "To tell you the truth, I really don't know. I haven't had any contact from them since the tires were slashed and they left that letter." She pulled out a chair and sat, her eyes on her mother. "I don't think it was them. It's not what I've come to expect from them."

"Are you saying there's someone else?" Anna drew in a deep breath, but before she could continue, Sloane spoke.

"There has to be. And I think it's about that man Shanley and I were asked to find and couldn't. The one those men were sure was Redmond." She buried her head in her folded arms. "Oh, what have I done? I've put Redmond at risk."

Sloane jumped as she felt an arm come around her and then heard Redmond's voice.

"Not at all, sweetheart. Not at all. They were after me, not you. You just happened to be there. But I don't understand who this Eric guy is."

"That's the thing, Redmond. There is no one by that name. Shamus looked. Your father looked. They can't find anyone by that name here in the area."

She raised her head, her eyes on him. "That's what's so bizarre, Redmond. Dad would have looked into it before he sent us out, at least a preliminary look."

"He did and what he found has disappeared."

She sighed before she pulled away and rose, stalking away. Redmond sat and watched her, unknown to him that his heart was on his face. The two mothers shared a look and a smile.

Redmond finally tracked Sloane down in the living room, curled up on the couch, an open book on her lap that he knew she hadn't been reading. He sat down beside her, his arm extended along the back of the couch, his fingers not quite touching her.

"Sloane?"

"I don't get it, Redmond. That's becoming my favourite phrase." She turned to him. "Who is after you?"

He shrugged. "We think it's related to an extraction we did a while ago that ended in tragedy. The lady was already dead when we got there. We think the local people set it up but we can't prove it. They've had to be working for someone here. All along we've thought someone has been after Dad, but we haven't been able to prove it, other than one family that we tracked down when Reilly was going through what he did."

"So, this is about your father? Why you, though?"

"Whoever it is has tried the other four. I'm the last, other than for Dad and Mom and I would rather whoever it was came after me, not them." He stared at the floor, unsure how to continue.

"What is it you want to ask?"

He grinned at her, knowing she was being blunt but that was her. Direct and to the point. "I'm not sure how to continue, but I worry about you."

"I know you do, but you're doing God's job."

"What do you mean?"

"You're trying to protect me, to wrap me in cotton, and keep me safe. It won't work. God is in control. He has allowed this over the years. You don't know the endless prayers I have uttered for it to be taken away, for the men to be caught somehow, that have never been answered. Until now."

Redmond looked up at that, catching a look on her face that stopped him from speaking for a moment, knowing that she had shown him her heart and that she cared for him, just as he did for her.

"Sloane?"

She shook her head. "Leave it, Redmond. We need to pray through our friendship, I think. I have no idea where all this is heading."

Sloane looked around around as she heard a sound and screamed, sending Redmond to his feet, his eyes on his mother as she was shoved into the room and down into a chair, a hand on her head keeping her there. Four men stood there, weapons pointed at the younger couple.

Chapter 12

Redmond tried to move towards his mother but was shoved back, losing his balance to fall on the couch. Sloane tried to move towards either Naomi or Redmond but her arm was caught in an iron grasp and she was pulled away from the both and towards the man who appeared to be the leader. She drew in a deep breath. She knew two of these men. They had been in the cave that day.

Her mind raced, trying to come up with a plan, watching as Redmond's arms were bound behind him and then a weapon held to his temple. He shook his head slightly at her, warning her to be careful.

She stared at the leader, her brow furrowed as she tried to place him. She knew him, she thought, just not how.

"Sloane, my dear. All these years. I can't say it's a pleasure." The man's smooth voice flowed out. She could tell he had cultivated the tone, it wasn't natural.

"I have no idea who you are or why you're here. I think you should just leave."

The man shook his head. "I don't think so. We need to come to an understanding, my dear."

"I am not your dear. Never have been. Never will be." That comment earned her a blow across her face, drawing blood from her lip, even as Redmond struggled to get to her.

"None of that, my dear. I think you misunderstood me. You have something I want."

She shook her head. "I don't. I never have."

"That's not what I've been told. That man that day? He had papers on him when he ran. They weren't on him when he was found. I have been told you were there, that you searched him and took them."

She shook her head, fear coursing through her for the first time. "I never had anything. No papers. Nothing. I just checked him, found him dead, and then hid when I heard the men coming. I didn't take anything from him." Her words were almost a sob as she saw the looks of hate and revenge on the man's face even as he advanced once more towards her, his hand up to deal her another blow, one she couldn't duck, that sent her down, her head hitting hard on the corner of the coffee table. She lay still, crumpled in a heap, her arms around her head in a protective manner.

Redmond gave a yell and sprang forward, despite the gun held on him and the bonds on his arms. His shoulders hit the man, knocking him back and to the ground. He vaguely heard his mother struggling and calling out to him before her voice was stopped by a gag.

He felt himself raised to his feet and was unable to stop or avoid the blows directed at him. He finally slumped to the floor, his vision blurred, pain driving all thoughts from his mind. He didn't hear the men arguing before they hurriedly left.

Naomi struggled to free herself but couldn't escape the ropes that bound her to the chair. Tears flowed down her cheeks, unstoppable as she watched her son lie there so still and then her glance went to Sloane, who too lay, unmoving. She shot a look at the clock and sighed. No one was expected home yet.   Riordan had a meeting that would likely run late he thought. The others had scattered, Rory and Leah back to their home at her bed and breakfast, Regan and Delaney to their home an hour away, Reilly was at the office with his father, and Ryanne and Shea had taken some time to fly to the Rockies to do a photo shoot he had been asked to do.

She finally looked up, her eyes on the clock. Two hours had passed, two hours she had spent in desperate prayer, her eyes shifting between the two on the floor. She heard the back door and then footsteps heading her way, Reilly's voice calling for her.

Reilly stopped in the doorway behind his mother, his mouth open to speak, when he sprang forward, his pocket knife out cutting at her bonds, tearing the gag from her mouth.

"Mom? What happened?"

"Call for help.   It's been over two hours now, Reilly.   We need help for Redmond and Sloane.   Please, Lord, let them be alive."

Reilly stood, not quite sure what his mother was saying, not having seen his brother or Sloane on the floor in the dimness of the light. He reached for the switches and then with an exclamation had his phone out, calling for help before he dropped it on the table and was beside Sloane, gentle hands feeling her, not daring to move her.

"Mom? Redmond?"

"He's alive, Reilly, but he took an awful beating. He tried to stop them from mistreating Sloane but she was already down." She looked around, shock giving way to determination. "How did you come to be here?"

He shrugged. "Dad sent me. He's on his way. He cut the conference short, said you needed him." He reached for his knife again to cut Redmond free. "What did they want?"

"The leader? I know him, but I can't think of his name right now. I'm too shaken. He said Sloane had papers. That she had taken them from a dead body years ago. She denied it." Naomi sat back on the floor. "What body?"

"She and one of her brothers had been out on a search for someone and found him dead. Sloane stayed with the body, she had her dog with her, and heard the men approaching. She hid, she thought, but she must have been seen by one of them. How do we find that out now?"

"Let your Dad work on that." She was on her feet and in her husband's arms as he almost ran into the room, following the emergency personnel who had responded.

Two hours later, Riordan paced his son's hospital room, his eyes shuttered. His heart hurt as he prayed. He had prayed that Redmond would be the one spared from what the others had faced. Naomi slept in a chair near her son. He knew Redmond would want to know how Sloane was. He turned as the door opened and William entered.

"You're Riordan Stuart?" William's hand was out to shake Riordan's.

"I am. I'm sorry we have to meet under these circumstances."

"Can't be helped. I need to thank your son. I understand he tried to help my daughter."

"He did." Riordan spun to stare at Redmond. "He's really battered. A lot of bruising. No broken bones." He turned back to William. "Sloane?"

"Concussion from where she hit the table. You didn't know that?" Riordan shook his head at that. "That's what I was told. Apparently the leader struck her enough to send her off balance and down. That's when Redmond tried to step in."

Riordan shook his head. "Naomi said they were after papers they think Sloane has?"

"Papers? What papers? She's never ever said anything at all."

"Apparently papers disappeared when she found that body all those years ago. Those are what they're after."

"From then? She never had anything. She changed after that. I blamed myself for sending her out and for her finding the body."

"It wasn't your fault. It's whoever she saw."

Chapter 13

Redmond stood the next day, his hands wrapped around the bedrail of Sloane's hospital bed, watching as she slept. He knew. He knew she was the one he had prayed for and been waiting for. That had become crystal clear the day before when she was attacked and sent to the floor. He thought she had died. He didn't want to lose her, but he wasn't sure how to approach her.

Sloane groaned as she moved, her head hurting as she turned it, her eyes flickering open to stare around the room. She groaned again. It was true then. That man had appeared. He had haunted her for years. She had forgotten she had seen him in the shadows that day, staying back but watching. She didn't know she had been seen.

She shifted, seeing hands gripping the railing and then raised her eyes, to find Redmond standing there, his eyes closed as he prayed. Her hand raised to touch his, bringing his eyes open again. His hand reached for her face, touching it gently.

"Sloane? How are you, sweetheart?"

"Sore. My head hurts and the room is spinning. How are you?"

He grinned. "I've been better. I was so afraid you were dead. I tried to get to you."

"I can see that. Redmond, what am I to do with you?"

"Marry me. I'm serious, Sloane."

"I can't. I'm too dangerous."

His finger on her mouth stopped her words. "So am I. What do you say? Want to be dangerous together?"

She stared at him, unable to shake her head, knowing it would make the pounding worse. "You know you're not to make decisions of this magnitude when you have a concussion?"

He smiled. "I think we had made this decision before that."

She sighed, a slight smile on her face. "Did we? I don't remember."

"We did." He reached to gently kiss her. "Will you?"

"Can I let you know yesterday?"

He stared at her for a moment, catching the grin she was trying to hide. "I can see I'm in for a fun time with you, sweetheart. So?"

"I will. Let's not wait. How long will you need to get ready?"

He stared at her against before he grinned. "I thought that was my line. I can be ready in an hour. How about you?"

"We need a license and a minister."

He held up his hand. "I have the application here. A friend will take me to the courthouse to get it. I just need your identification. And then we need to find a minister."

"Try John Withers. He's a retired minister who still does ceremonies. I would like him."

He nodded, turned to leave and then turned back, reaching to kiss her again. "You're sure?"

"I am, Redmond. Someone once told me it didn't matter about all the trappings of a wedding, who was there, or things like that. Anyone could have a wedding. It was the marriage that mattered."

"Whoever that was, was wise."

She watched him walk away and then stared at her hospital gown. She was not getting married in that. She reached for her phone, hesitating on who to call, finally calling her mother.

"Mom? You're heading back here?"

"We are. We're just about to leave. Did you want something?"

"I do, Mom." Tears sparkled on her cheeks for a moment, before she wiped at them. "Your wedding dress."

"Sloane? My wedding dress? What are you talking about?"

"I need it, Mom and I need it today. I know it will fit. You've told me I'm about your size."

"Oh, Sloane, you didn't."

"Didn't what? Get engaged? I did. We're getting married soon. Redmond's gone to get the license."

"Oh, honey. Are you sure?"

"I am, Mom. I need this. He makes me feel so safe and loved and special."

"Then, I will bring it. We'll be there in about thirty minutes."

Redmond stood beside Reilly, who was staring at him. "Are you crazy? You're rushing into this."

Redmond began to laugh, his finger pointed at Reilly, who finally grinned. "I have to eat those words, don't I?"

"You do. I'm sure Aideen thought you were crazy."

"I know she did. At the time, I knew I loved her but she wasn't sure about anything, let alone me. Now you tell me you and Sloane love each other. Then, God's blessing you on, Redmond. You always have marched to a different drummer than the rest of us."

Redmond laughed even harder, causing his father to spin around and stare at his sons. "Dad would say that about us all, I think."

Chapter 14

Two days later, Redmond watched as Sloane slept, her face showing the pain she was feeling. He wanted to make it all better for her but couldn't. Shanley had been by, talking to his sister, trying to get her to go back to the hospital for more testing. She had simply told him to shut up and if he couldn't do that, the door was at the front of the house. He knew where to find it.

Redmond had been shocked at her words, knowing he would never have heard them from his own sisters, but had grinned as Shanley had just laughed and hugged his sister. She had slapped him on the arm before she hugged him back.

He turned as he heard footsteps approaching. His mother had stopped by, with food. She said they had enough to do, trying to recover without having to worry about cooking. Her hand rested briefly on his head before she sat, her eyes on him.

"Redmond?"

"Mom, where do I go from here? I mean, with the investigation? Has Dad found out anything yet?"

"He hasn't said. I know he's working on it. Shamus asked if he could work with your Dad and the two of them and Reilly are deep into it. I know Regan and Rory are as well. Ryanne I haven't heard from yet."

He sighed. "I want this over. It's haunted her for long enough."

"I know you do. Each one of the others said the same thing at some point or other." She pointed at Sloane. "She needs to heal. You need to let her. You need to heal yourself. Let others work through this for now. You two need to take care of one another." She looked down for a moment and then back up. "I'm proud of the man you've become. I know I've said it before, son, but you are a true example to the rest of us." She rose, bending to drop a kiss on his head and then leaving.

Redmond sat, his thoughts muddled before he heard the doorbell and rose. Now who, he wondered? He stopped, his hand on the open door before he reached to hug the woman standing there and shake the man's hand.

"Abe? Emma? What are you two doing there? Come in. I'm in the living room. Sloane's still sleeping."

"We heard. God's blessings on you two. Abe, here. Take this. I'm raiding the kitchen. I hear Naomi left food."

Redmond simply grinned as he pointed to a seat for Abe, taking the chair he had been in, his eyes on Sloane as she stirred slightly at the noise and then settled back down.

"I need to wake her shortly. Tell me why you're here."

"You."

Redmond stared at Abe and then at Emma as she entered a tray in her hands that Abe rose to take from her.

"Yes, you. And her." Abe pointed at Sloane. "We have news we needed to share with you. We just weren't expecting to find you two had married."

"We did. We decided we didn't want to wait. But what news do you have?"

"Eat first, Redmond. Can she eat as well?"

"She can but she's not sure she wants to." Sloane had awakened and sat up, pain briefly crossing her face. "Redmond, please introduce me."

"Sloane, this is Abe Finlay and his wife, Emma. She's the one I told you about."

"The one? Who? Which one? You've talked about so many people, I can't keep them straight."

Emma was watching and caught the glint of mischief in the other woman's eyes, fighting back her laughter at the sight.

Redmond stared at Sloane, not quite sure of what she was saying, before his eyes narrowed and he smirked.

"I have talked a lot, haven't I? Emma's the one I said could find out anything."

"Oh, right. That's her. I think I remember now." She looked at the tray. "Feed me, husband."

Abe and Emma broke out into laughter as Redmond stared at Sloane before he too grinned. "See, Abe, I'm henpecked after only two days."

"I doubt that very much." Abe reached for the plate of sandwiches, serving the others before he helped himself.

Emma finally reached for the large envelope she had set on the floor near her chair and handed it to Redmond. "In there, you'll find a summary of what I've found so far. I'm still researching but have gotten pulled into something else that has had to take priority."

"That's fine, Emma." Redmond stared at the envelope, his hand running over it. "Do I want, sorry, do we want to know what's in here?"

Emma nodded even as Abe spoke. "You do. It concerns both of you. And somehow both threads of our investigation connect the two. Somewhere along the line, Redmond, both your father and Sloane's father made the same enemy."

"They did?" Sloane shifted her body, her head down on Redmond's shoulder. "How?"

"That we haven't quite got the answer on yet. We're working through the names we've found. But I can tell you the men are very dangerous. What you went through? That's just a small sample of what they can and will do. You need to be very vigilant. It may mean the difference between life and death for either of you, both of you, or a family member."

Redmond reached to lay Sloane down on the couch, covering her with a blanket before he sat once more, her feet on his knee. "How do we do that?"

"That's why Abe is here. He has some suggestions for you. He also wants Joseph, our security system expert, to go through each of your homes. I know you and your family have excellent systems. We just want to make sure they can't be hacked into or taken down."

"That works." Redmond sat for a moment. "Other suggestions?"

Abe grinned. "Well, Ian did offer to fly you two somewhere you couldn't be found."

Redmond shouted with laughter at that, causing Sloane to shift slightly in her sleep. "He's still doing that?"

"He is. I'm afraid his daughter will have a time of it when she begins to date." Abe was grinning at the thought.

"I'm sure she will. He teases but has such a heart of gold."

Chapter 15

A week later, her headaches now subsiding, Sloane wandered her new home, taking in the decoration and the furnishings. Redmond had told her to make what changes she wanted, but she had declined. This was his home and she felt a stranger here, even though she now lived in it as Redmond's wife.

She turned as she heard her phone, looking for it and not finding it. She finally tracked it down in the kitchen, scrolling through her messages, laughing at the ones from her brothers, a softened expression on her face at the ones from Redmond, and then freezing at the last one. She dropped her phone as if it had burned her and sprang back, hitting the wall behind her, sliding down to sit, her arms around her abdomen, her eyes on the counter where her phone lay.

Redmond found her there late that afternoon, his jacket and briefcase hitting the floor as he crouched beside her before he sat, pulling her to him, cradling her to him as she began to shake.

"Sloane?   Sweetheart?   What happened?"

"They've found my cell number. There's a text message on it.   Redmond, please! Make them stop!"

He stared at the counter she had pointed to, and then wrapped her tighter in his arms. "I can't, sweetheart, as much as I would like to. I just can't. I'll get you a new phone with a number no one knows."

"That won't work.   That number should not have been in the public numbers. It's unlisted."

Redmond's face grew grimmer. "Then we'll figure out something so that you have a phone without them finding your number."

She finally struggled to rise, Redmond watching before he too stood, walking over to her phone, activating the screen and scrolling through the messages. More than one had come in and each one was more disturbing than the previous one. He turned to her, to find her watching him closely.

"Do we need to leave town, Redmond? Can we even do that?"

"We can. I know of a cabin I can get. It's ours but not too many people know where it is. It would mean a hike of a bit but I'm not sure you're up to that."

"My headaches are better. Can we leave in the morning?"

"We can. Go, pack what you need. And find what I need as well. The packs are in the spare room closet." He had his phone out as she ran from the room. "Hello, Dad? We're leaving in the morning. No, I don't want to say where we're heading. You know where. The thing of it is, they've found her cell number. There have been quite a few nasty messages. What's that? I'll leave it on the counter for you. A vehicle? I thought of them tracking us. I know one I can get that's not associated with us. You know who to call if you need to reach us."

He cut his father's voice off, not wanting to say any more, but knowing his father understood and would be there in the morning to retrieve Sloane's phone and search it. Redmond reached for another pack, looking through the pantry for the dehydrated food he kept, reaching for the water treatment he carried when he hiked, checking his pack to make sure he had enough supplies to last. He reached for his own phone, this time sending off a text to Abe, asking for a ride in the morning. Abe's response was immediate, stating simply to meet him at a diner nearby and they would be taken on their way.

Sloane stood for a moment watching Redmond, before she was across the room and in his arms, her head burrowed as tight to him as she could get.

"You got us packed?"

"I did. I hope I took the right stuff. I hate this, Redmond."

"I know you do. So do I. I talked to Dad. He'll pick up your phone. He'll need your password."

"Let me change it to something he would know."

"No. Leave yours. Just let him know what it is."

She nodded, knowing he had a reason for asking that. "What about a ride? We can't leave a vehicle wherever for long in the winter."

"No, we can't. I talked to Abe. He's arranging for a ride for us. In fact, I would not be surprised to have company with us to the cabin, just to make sure we get there."

"He'd do that?"

"He would, Sloane. It's what he does. Provide security. Although now he trains others to do that."

"But he would do that for you?"

"He would. He knows how we need to get away until plans can be put in place. You didn't see the rest of the messages, did you?"

Her face paled. "There was more than one?"

"There was. Each one was more vicious and sickening then the first." He looked around. "We need to eat."

"I'm not hungry." She reached for the kettle, intent on making herself a hot chocolate.

"I'm not either. There's some soup. Can you eat some at least for me?"

She finally nodded. "I will if you will."

Redmond's heart broke for his young bride, knowing they were just beginning their walk in danger. What they had already faced? He knew from experience it would be nothing compared to what they could and would face. He prayed for protection for them both and for those researching and seeking answers for them.

Chapter 16

Pulling her hat down closer over the hair she had tucked up under it and tightening the scarf around her neck, Sloane finally tucked her hands into her pockets, watching as Redmond paced in front of her. His car was near them, and she knew he was anxious to be underway, not liking having either one of them in the open like they were. A truck finally pulled up close to them and stopped, the doors opening as two men around Redmond's age dropped down to the pavement and approached him, hands extended to shake his. They spoke for a moment, before they walked towards her.

Redmond's arm around her, he turned her to the men. "Sweetheart, this is Luke and Micah. Abe sent them."

"Abe did, did he? Thank you. I hate putting you in danger."

Luke laughed as Micah simply grinned.

"It's what we do, Sloane. It's who we are. Redmond, your packs?" Micah turned to him.

"I left them somewhere last night. I'll tell you where once we're on the way."

"Smart thinking. Now, the keys to your car? You left them inside?"

"I did. Tom at the diner has them. Reilly will pick it up later for me and take it to the business to give it a good going over."

Luke nodded. "That's a wise move although I know you do that weekly. Now, let's get you two out of sight."

Four hours later, Sloane gratefully dropped her pack on the floor of the small cabin before she wandered around it. It was nice, she thought, compact. She turned as the door opened and Redmond entered, pulling off his hat and then just standing inside the door, hesitation in his matter, his eyes watchful as he took in the room and then Sloane.

"Sloane?"

"Redmond?" She moved into his hug. "Thank you. I needed to get away. I have for months."

"And you didn't."

She shook her head. "It's too hard to explain to the men of my family that I need space and have needed it for months. Having to move back in with Shanley while my house is repaired was really tough."

"I am sure it was. I realized with Ryanne how tough it was, having older brothers who wanted to take over for her." He turned her to face the cabin. "This is small, but we tried to put in everything we could think of. There's no power, but we have lots of lamps and fuel for them. I was up here a month or so ago and split and piled lots of wood, so that's not a problem." He was worried all of a sudden, that this had been a bad move.

"We'll be fine, Redmond. We will be just fine." She moved away, reaching for one of the packs with their supplies. "We're here for what, a week, ten day?"

"Something like that. I told Dad two weeks."

She nodded, her hand rubbing against the wooden countertop. "That's fine." She was distracted, thoughts tumbling through her mind, a headache growing in intensity. She felt Redmond's hands on her shoulders before he scooped her up and stepped over to the bunk, laying her down, tugging off her boots and then tucking her under the covers.

"Sleep, sweetheart. The headache won't go away unless you do." He bent to drop a kiss on her temple and then stepped away, quietly putting their supplies away before he turned to stand beside the bunk, one hand braced against the wall, the other clenched in anger as he studied Sloane, knowing she was hurting and that for once he couldn't make it better for her.

Sloane stirred in the late afternoon, her eyes opening as she studied the cabin before they lit on Redmond seated at the table, papers spread out in front of him. She rose and silently padded to stand beside him, her hand on his shoulder, before his arm came around her.

"How's the head?"

"It's still there but better. What are you working on? I thought you left all this at the office." She moved a paper with a slim fingertip.

"I couldn't. I mean, I didn't want to. I want to figure out who is after us, if I can. I thought maybe we could talk about it while we're here."

"Not today, Redmond. I need a break from all this."

He watched as she headed into the kitchenette before he sighed and looked down at his work. He was making progress, that he knew. He had drawn up a family tree of sorts for the murdered man and was working out from there. He was scared, he admitted to himself. This was way above what any of then suspected.

A week later, refreshed by the change, Sloane laughed as Redmond tried to pack his papers away without crinkling them.

"Not working for you?"

He frowned at her even as mischief danced in his eyes. "It did when I came here."

She shoved him aside, tidied up the papers and smoothly slid them into his pack. "There you go. Now, what time are we leaving?"

"Now." He looked out the window. "This time, it's Luke and Abe. I'm not liking that Abe is here."

"And why not?"

"Because it could mean bad news." He walked out of the cabin on those words, leaving Sloane staring after him before she shook her head, hastening to finish packing and then reaching for her jacket, even as the door opened and the men entered.

Abe stood for a moment, his eyes on Sloane, before he shook his head. How did he tell her that they had received increasing threats, that leaving town had not changed that? That her family was now being threatened? He had talked to each of them and gave advice but he knew it didn't always work the way they thought it would.

"Abe? If you're here, it has to be bad news." Sloane went directly to the point.

Abe laughed. "Still direct, I see. I wouldn't say bad news but concerning news."

She leaned against the counter, her hands worrying her hat. "They've threatened my family, haven't they? Of course, they have. They always do, don't they? Trying to bring me to terms. But I don't have anything they want. I took nothing from the body. If papers are missing, then he hid them somewhere years ago. And I have no idea where."

Abe nodded. "We know that. They know that. They're trying to scare you but there's more. This is escalating into something much deeper, Redmond. Sloane. Whatever happened in the past, it links your families."

"You've said that before, Abe. Why?" Redmond had moved to stand beside Sloane, an arm around her.

"That's the word on the street. We're working to verify it. So are your local police forces. For now, let's get you two home. Luke, you're first. Sloane, you're next. Redmond. And I'll bring up the rear." Abe stared at Redmond until he nodded, reaching for their packs.

Sloane paced the house before she slumped to the couch, a frown on her face. It was late evening, they had been home for hours and she was bored, she thought. No, not bored, more worried than she wanted anyone to know. How did she solve this? How did she keep her family and more importantly, her husband, safe?

Redmond watched, his heart breaking for his wife, knowing they were not finished with the men. He feared for what was ahead, having seen how things escalated with his siblings, and knowing the stories of Abe and his friends. He turned back to his office, a thought running through his mind, jotting a quick note, before he turned out the lights and headed to find Sloane.

Chapter 17

Redmond was on a hunt for his father, not finding him anywhere in the office building. He stopped in the kitchen area, his hand rubbing at the back of his neck, not sure where to head next. He turned as he heard his name called, Reilly running towards him.

"Redmond. I just got word. Dad's been in an accident."

"Accident? How bad?"

"His car is totalled. He was being taken to the hospital. He was worried about you and Sloane."

Redmond snorted. "Of course he would be. He never thinks of himself. Sloane's in my office. Let's detour by there." He stopped as Sloane ran towards her, fear on her face. "Sloane?"

"Redmond! It's my parents. They were in an accident. I don't know how bad."

Redmond stopped her with hands on her arms. "Reilly, who called about Dad?"

"The police". He paused, catching where Redmond was heading with his question. "You don't think? Of course, you do." He turned as he heard footsteps behind. "And here is Dad."

Riordan stopped, frowning, as his gaze shifted between his sons. "What is going on?"

Redmond held up a finger, as he spoke into the phone. "William, you and Anna are fine? No, she's fine. She just received a message that you two were in an accident." He listened for a moment, his arms tight around Sloane. "I agree. It was a ploy to get us out from here. Stay safe. We'll be by later. Or better still, meet us at Dad's. That works. We'll see you then."

Riordan's face was stern as he listened to the explanations given him. "They really want to get their hands on you. Redmond, to use you more than likely against Sloane. Sloane, because they think you have something."

She shook her head. "This is not making sense, Riordan. Not at all. They know there aren't any papers. So why?"

"Why? That's a good question, one we don't have the answers to yet."

"And we need to. We need to think this through." Sloane paced, her hands pressed to her temples. "Where do we start? And with whom?"

Redmond shook his head as he grinned at his father. "You've started something, Dad. She'll not sleep or rest until she solves it."

Sloane spun at his words, before she shook a finger at him. "Behave yourself, Mr. Stuart. This means work for you as well." She turned to Reilly. "I need a topographical map of this area, pens, highlighters, markers, paper."

"And the kitchen sink?" Reilly waited, knowing at some point she would hear him.

"And that too. It may be the one piece we've been overlooking." She caught at Redmond's hand, a distracted look on her face before she winked at him, causing him to choke back his laughter.

Sloane, you're good for us. Reilly didn't see that coming. He walked way from his family, heading for the conference room.

Reilly stared after them, his mouth open before he snapped it closed, turning to his father, finding a huge grin on that man's face. He finally just shook his head.

"I don't think anyone has ever replied quite like that."

Riordan laughed even harder. "No, I don't they have." He was finally able to control his laughter enough to reply. "Not even Aideen has been able to stop you in your tracks with a response to that one."

Redmond watched Sloane for a while, standing back before he moved to a place beside her, his hand reaching to stop hers.

"Sloane, talk to us. Tell us what you're looking for or hoping to find."

She sighed. "I'm sorry. I'm just so used to working out searches like this. We work it through and then share." She looked up, her eyes thoughtful. "This is how I'm working this. As a grid search." She pointed to the map that she had used string to section off. "Each section has to be searched. It'll take a long time."

"Not necessarily." Redmond perched on the table with one hip, his foot idly swinging. "Where do you find the man?"

She looked over the map and finally pointed to a section. "He was here. We came in from this way. I think his path was tracked backwards but I'm not even sure that was done."

"Dad's asking for a report. He's homing to have it tonight or by tomorrow." He studied Sloane, seeing the fatigue on her face. "Sloane, we need to stop for the night."

"I can't."

"No, you can't. It's that you won't." He reached to gently take the pen from her hand and then taking her hand, led her from the room, stopping to lock the door behind him. "We're set up here in the apartment. Dad didn't want us out and about as he put it."

"You have an apartment here?"

"We do. We set it up for the ladies we brought out, so they had somewhere to decompress and rest, if that was what they wanted. Now that we're not doing that, Dad has said we'll use it for family if there's a need. And right now, that's us. I slipped home with Regan and brought us some stuff."

"Stuff? Is that what it's called? I've designating it as clothes and personal items all along? That's my problem. I just don't know what to call anything anymore." She stopped abruptly, a thought running through her mind.

"Sloane?" Redmond tugged her into movement once more. "What's going on in that mind of yours?"

She shrugged. "I am not sure. Just an impression. Redmond? I need you to find me some verses, verses that will help get us through."

"I can do that. Mom left some food for us. We'll eat and then do just that." He hugged her, feeling her trembling, knowing that they were working towards something neither of them wanted to face but they had no choice in.

Chapter 18

Sloane studied her work the next morning, the thought still hovering near the edge of her mind without being clear. She knew it was the answer. Just how she knew that, she didn't understand. Redmond stood beside her, an arm around her, holding out a mug of hot chocolate for her. She took it in a distracted manner, not hearing Riordan and her father enter the room.

William watched for a while before he walked over, studying what she had done so far. She's good, he thought. She's always been able to plan out our searches in a logical sequential way. His head tilted as he looked over the map before he pointed to a section.

"There. Did that area get searched? It's not too far off the trail that we think the man took."

"That area? That's one I was thinking of, Dad. We need to search it only it's winter and been so many years."

"I know, love. I know. We may not find anything but it's worth a trip out there. Any other areas?"

He watched as she pointed to a number. "That's quite a few."

"I know, Dad. I'm just not content about them. They don't seem to fit, not with what we know of the area. He may have hidden what they're looking for in town too."

"That's true. Unfortunately, the authorities were never able to track where he came from. He had no identification on him. He's remained a John Doe."

"I don't like that, Dad. He should have been named."

"I know, Sloane. I know. It's just he never was."

Redmond finally spoke. "He not likely was from this area, then. Reilly, did we look back at any missing persons' reports from then from outside the area and the country?"

"We did, but I'll take another look. Emma or Jace was working on that as well. They have resources and contacts we don't."

Late that afternoon, Reilly found Redmond, sitting at a table in the conference room, his eyes on his work. He slid into a seat beside him, a mug of coffee set in front of his brother.

"How's Sloane?"

Redmond looked up, a bleak look around his eyes. "She's hurting, Reilly, in more ways than one. I finally made her lie down, her headache was bad. She fought me on that, but right now she's sleeping." He glanced towards the cot where she lay. "This is destroying her, Reilly. I want it over."

"It's been coming for years. God knows why you are going through this." He sipped at his own coffee before he spoke again. "Emma called."

"She called? Didn't just sent the material?"

"No, she felt she had too. Abe is wanting to send his team. Dad asked that they wait for now. He feels you're safe enough here, for now."

"But we can't stay here forever, that's a given. Sloane will run if we try and keep her caged for too long."

"And you'll be right with her. I know that feeling, Redmond, given what Aideen and I went through." He looked down at the papers he had dropped. "I made some notes but she promised to send on her research." He paused, not sure how to continue.

"She found the man and named him?"

"She did. He was from Alberta, here on a business trip. His family have searched for years. For some reason, and that reason I would like to know, his photo and description never made it past our officers here. It was buried in a closed file."

"That's a shame." He sat back. "So it was never shared with the provincial force or any other force. Why?"

"That's what we're trying to find out. Dad knows the detective who was working on it. He always questioned his integrity but never had enough to go to anyone about him. He had problems with him when they were teens and could never understand why that man went on the force."

"Not another one." Redmond's head sank into his hands. "Where does it stop, Reilly? How deep does this go? And how does it involve William?"

"That we don't know. William moved here when the kids were small, Sloane just a few months old, and stared up his backpacking company and from that, he was asked to set up a search and rescue organization, which he gladly did." Reilly searched his notes. "Emma says that William had conflict as well with that detective, being falsely accused of fraud."

"That's our connection then. This detective. Where is he now?"

"That we don't know and we're trying to determine. He left the force about five years ago under a cloud. We're not sure where he ended up."

"He likely assumed a different name or moved from the area." Redmond rose and walked to study the map. "Sloane keeps focusing on a certain area here, Reilly. She says there are some depressions and almost cave-like openings. She wants to go out there and search."

"Not a good idea. They're waiting just for that." Reilly stood shoulder to shoulder with his brother. "Why don't you two take off and visit Regan or Rory?"

Redmond shook his head. "No. Sloane is adamant she doesn't want to bring any more harm to our family or hers than has already happened. She's scared, Reilly. No, let me re-phrase that. She's terrified, has been for years. I want this man, the one behind all this. She can't begin to heal until this is over. I catch glimpses of the freedom she's gradually finding, but I want more of that for her. I love the woman she is when she's like that."

"Like she was with her comment about the kitchen sink?" Reilly grinned as Redmond began to laugh.

"She got you on that one, didn't she? You have to watch your words. She's good at the comebacks."

"So I see." Reilly focused on the map, his finger tracing the route the police thought the man had taken. "If that detective hid information, what's to say he didn't send the search officers off on a wrong track?"

"That's what Sloane is working on, trying to find other paths he could have taken. Did the report say anything about a vehicle?"

Reilly shook his head. "No, and there should have been. Dad's looking into that. We suspect he had a rental car and that the car was taken back to the rental company. I doubt we can track that now."

"Not likely. And if he was from out of the province, he would have flown in." Redmond sighed. "This is not easy." He looked around as he felt a hand touch him. "Sloane? I thought you were sleeping."

"I was but I've been having this weird dream." She nodded to Reilly. "What if this man had no connection to what was going on? He just happened to be there. That he wasn't murdered but had a health crisis and died naturally. Did you ever pull the coroner's report?"

"Sloane!" Reilly's exclamation caused her to grin. "What did you just go and do?"

"I think I solved the mystery of the man. If I remember someone reported the car sitting there for a day and Dad was asked to search.   If he had been involved in something, it is not likely the car would have still sat there."

Redmond stared at her before he pointed to her.   "That's what has been bothering me. The call. Who made it?"

She shrugged.   "A farmer.   He had been driving by between his properties. When it hadn't moved, he called Dad. Dad sent Shamus and I in to look."

They all looked around as Riordan entered, flipping through the papers in his hands.   "Sloane?   That man you found? Heart attack.   He had heart disease.   The original coroner's report states it was natural causes." He looked up, surprised to see the three of them staring at him.

"Thanks, Dad.   That's what we were just discussing.   Natural causes.   That doesn't explain the men who were there."

"No, it doesn't.   Unless he saw or heard something he shouldn't have, and that we will never know." Riordan stared down at the map, a frown on his face. "So, that closes that chapter. Where do we stand?"

"Looking down at a map that's not talking." Sloane walked away, leaving Redmond and Reilly laughing at the expression on their father's face.

Riordan stared after her, before he shook his head, a smile on his face. "She's good, Redmond. You have to be on your toes around her."

"That you do, Dad. That you do."

Chapter 19

A week had passed since Riordan had walked into the conference room and Redmond watched Sloane carefully. She was pale, losing weight, and he hated that. He finally just packed her up and drove away from the building, not telling her where they were heading. He stopped finally at a small cabin on the Lake Erie Shore, far enough away from the town they lived in he prayed that they would be safe.

Sloane stood for a moment, her eyes on the cabin before she turned them to Redmond, narrowing them at his grin.

"Redmond? Why?"

"Why? Because you need a break from your research. You won't take it if we stay there. We need some us time."

She sighed as she walked into his hug. "How long?"

"Just until Saturday. Three days. That's all. Isn't that long enough?"

135

She swatted his arm as she moved towards the cabin, finding him before her to open the door. "Is this really safe?"

"It should be. Abe found it for me."

"Of course he did. What can't he do?"

Redmond laughed at that. "A lot but he is very concerned about this. Emma's not finding what she should be on the men and that's worrying her. Ian wanted to fly us away somewhere safe and not tell anyone where we were."

"He threatens that?"

"He does. He does with every lady in distress and danger." Redmond poked wood into the stove and lit it before he turned to the fireplace and did the same. "Emma said the cabin was stocked with food and she had Abe bring in some fresh stuff for us."

"We are going to owe them so much when we're finsihed." She stared as Redmond shook his head. "What? Of course, we will."

"They'll never let you pay. That's a given. It's who they are. They do this for God, as a service for Him."

"Oh." She walked away from him, searching the cabin, noting the nice décor, the two bedrooms, a compact bathroom, before she dropped her pack in the nearest room. "This is nice." She walked back towards him and into his hug. "That's a great way to look at it, service for God. That's how your family does it."

"It is. Now that we're changing what we do, we still do that. It's keeping all of us involved, even Regan who tried hard to resign."

"She didn't, did she?"

Redmond nodded. "She did. She didn't want to travel anymore and she didn't think there was anything at the office she could do. Now, she can work remotely from their home and only come in if she really needs to."

Sloane nodded, content to be held by the man she loved, and content knowing he would do all he could to protect her.

On the following Monday, Redmond stood once more in the conference room, ready to fight through to find the ones responsible. His father had stopped him on the way by, stating that they needed to talk and he needed Sloane there. Shamus was on his way in. He had called in the early morning hours that he had found information. What that information was, he didn't say, just that he needed to meet with his father, Riordan and whoever else was around.

Sloane stared at her brother as he finished speaking. "There is no way Old Man Greene is involved. Why would he report the car if he was?"

Shamus shrugged. "I have no idea. And we can't ask him. He's disappeared. I spoke with his son last night, just wanting to go back over that day with his father, and Ryan said his father told him he was taking a vacation."

"Vacation? He never does that. Why now?"

"Likely because he is scared and he knows the whole thing is unraveling." Riordan looked up at that point. "From what I can see, he's been close to the legal line on many occasions. Now, he's wanted as a material witness in a new case and he doesn't want to be questioned. Any ideas where he would go?"

Sloane moved back towards them. "You know, I used to hear rumours that he had a second place, a cabin back in the woods." She stared down at the map and pointed. "Right here." She sighed. "And of course, it would be near where that body was found. Are we never to be free of that?"

Riordan followed her finger. "It is close to there. What was the name of the farmer again?"

"Greene."

Redmond heard his father draw in a deep breath and spun to stare at him, finding his father's eyes on William, who looked startled as well.

"Greene? Him? It's been him?" William walked away from them, his hand rubbing at his neck.

"I would think so, William. That's the tie between us. I had a run-in with him years ago. I suspect you did too."

"I did, both when we were in our twenties. I thought we had moved past that."

"Obviously not. He's kept watch all these years, waiting for the right time. He thought to get to you through Sloane. And to me through Rory and Regan and that last extraction that went so bad."

"Dad, what are you two talking about?" Sloane stared at her father, not sure where he was going with his statement.

"He's the one that didn't want me to start the search and rescue. He claimed someone was missing, only they weren't. He wanted to take the glory of finding them, only we showed him up as lying. He's never forgiven that, I guess. It happened when you were just a baby, Sloane."

Chapter 20

Redmond finally turned from his computer, his eyes on Sloane as she sat across the desk from her, her eyes closed, her head bowed. He knew her Bible was open on her knee. He had seen that when he had been on his feet hours ago. He rose, walked around the desk, and set the Bible on the desk before he scooped her up in his arms and sat back down, cradling her close.

She looked up, startled for a moment, before she smiled, her head coming down on his shoulder.

"All done for the day?"

He shook his head. "I'm running some searches that will take a few minutes. I just needed to talk to you."

"And you couldn't do that from across your desk?" She pointed to his chair, mischief sparkling on her face.

"No, I couldn't. I couldn't steal kisses from my wife if I was over there." He watched, delighted, as she blushed at that.

"Enough, Redmond. What have you found?"

He shook his head. "First, what did you find? You seem more at peace now."

"I am. I've been reading back through all the verses I could find that showed God's provision and protection for us. There are a lot. I realized how important we are to him."

"We are. He cares for us in a way we really don't comprehend." Redmond studied the desk, his thoughts mixed. "I'm not sure I can even explain how I think of that."

"I don't think we're supposed to. We accept it and move on. We don't try and explain how our earthly fathers care for us. We can't do that with God. He's just too big and awesome."

"That He is." Redmond sat for a few minutes, his fingers moving her rings before he spoke. "Dad called a while ago. He says there have been new threats. Pictures of us out and about. Pictures of our families. Pictures of our homes and vehicles."

"Of course, there is. It's what they do, right? Threaten us and when that doesn't work, they move on to the families. They want us unsettled and scared."

"And I have been at times. So have you, but you're not now. Don't run ahead of us, that's all I ask."

She studied him, her hand on his cheek before she shook her head. "I won't. I need my protector with me. But where do we go? We can't just sit around and wait for the next shoe to drop, as Mom would say."

"No, we can't. I've been thinking through some options that we'll need to pray through, I suspect. We'll talk about them later. Right now, Mom has said she's expecting us in the kitchen for a family meal. That is, if you want."

She studied him and then was off his knee and out the door, running for the kitchen, knowing he would be right behind her. And she was right. She heard his shout of laughter and then his footsteps behind her.

Naomi looked around as Sloane flew into the kitchen, sliding to a stop beside her, before she looked at Redmond as he stopped in the doorway, a grin on his face. Thank you, Lord. You have provided the lady he needs to bring back the fun to his life. He had become way too serious, given what we do and given what his siblings have been through.

"Hungry, are we?" was her only comment, earning her a hug from Sloane and a nod from Redmond.

Sloane had eaten without realizing what she had on her plate, her mind searching and thinking. She abruptly rose, her meal unfinished, and almost ran from the room. Redmond watched and went to rise, his mother's hand on his arm as she shook her head, rising to follow the younger woman. She found her in the conference room, staring down at the map.

An arm around her, Naomi waited, finally speaking.

"Sloane? What did you remember?"

Sloane shook her head, tears on her cheeks. "I don't cry. Do you know that? I do not cry."

"But at some point, we all do. God gave us tears for healing as well as sorrow."

Sloane sighed. "I know that. I'm just tired of crying. Redmond doesn't know how often I have."

"He knows, my dear. He just doesn't say anything. That's when he'll just hold you and cry with you, even though you don't see his tears."

Sloane had turned her head to study Naomi. "Is that what Riordan does?"

"He does. And I suspect your father does the same with your mother. Want to talk about it?"

Sloane shrugged, a finger moving over the map. "I'm missing something, Naomi. Something big and I don't know what."

"I know you'll have prayed about that. That's who you are and what you do. Talk to me. What do you think you have missed?"

Sloanse shrugged, not seeing Redmond hovering in the doorway, concerned about her.

"I'm not sure. I just don't know what it is. It's something or someone."

"Would it help if you walked back through that area?"

She shrugged once more. "I doubt it. We were back there about six momths ago. Everything is so changed." Her voice died away as a thought struck her. "That's what it is. There was a huge old oak tree. It's come down. Now, I wonder?"

"You wonder if there was something in it? How be we set out tomorrow and see what we can find? Riordan will go. I know your Dad will. Shamus will want to. So will Reilly. Now, Redmond, I understand he has to stay here and work very diligently on his paperwork. He's behind on that."

Sloane grinned at the laughter in Naomi's voice, having guessed that Redmond was behind her.

"He does, does he? Then, I guess we'll have to leave him here in the office while we go out on a field trip."

She giggled as his arms came around her, bringing laughter to his mother's face.

"Not without me, you don't."

Chapter 21

Shamus paced around the fallen tree the next morning, his eyes on it before he lifted them to Sloane, who stood, first looking at the tree and then spinning to search the surround area.

"Sloane? What are you thinking? And I know you are."

"This tree. It's larger than I remember even from three years ago."

"Time has a way of changing our perspective. And it will look bigger on the ground than when it was upright." Shamus leaned on it, his eyes assessing it before he frowned. "There. On your side, Sloane. It looks like a knot hole that is really big."

She nodded, her hands reaching for it before Redmond's hands stopped her. She turned her face to him in a frown.

"No, you don't reach into that. You let one of us." Redmond refused to back down, finally moving Sloane away from the tree trunk as Reilly and Shamus moved it. He stood, his arm around her, her father behind her, Riordan beside her. He knew others of their associates stood around, backs to them, watchful for any trouble. This would be a prime time to take one of them out.

Reilly's hand reached deep into the hole as he felt around. "It's too deep to reach the bottom. Dad, we brought an axe, didn't we?"

Shamus reached to take it, his eyes on Reilly as the younger man moved back, before he struck at the trunk, chips and chunks of wood flying from the blade, before he stopped and stood back, letting Reilly once more reach into the hole.

"Can you now reach the bottom?" Shams stood, axe in hand, ready to work away if Reilly needed him to.

"I can. It's just that whatever is down here is stuck. It feels like a metal box of some kind."

"Let me there again. I'll see how far down I can get with the axe before I hit it."

The two men worked away before Reilly was finally able to free the small tin box. He handed it to Sloane, watching the emotions work across her face, before she looked up at him.

"Do you remember this box, Shamus?"

He nodded, compassion on his face. "Gramps gave you that. It disappeared years ago."

"It did. About the time the body was found. I searched and searched for it. How did it end up here?"

Riordan spoke up. "Is there anything else in there?"

Reilly had been looking and raised his head. "Nothing, Dad. Absolutely nothing." He turned to watch Sloane. "I would suggest we head back for the office before we open that."

Riordan nodded, motioning for them to move out. Sloane walked forward, tripping over debris in front of her, not seeing where she was heading, Redmond's arm around her.

They finally stood in the conference room, the box down on paper on a table, Sloane standing in front of it, her arms wrapped around her. Shamus and Shanley stood on either side of her, her father behind her. Redmond stood to one side, knowing she needed her brothers there, a history shared between them regarding that box.

She finally reached out a finger to trace the box, the rust dropping away in places.

"Shanley? You open it. You're the oldest."

He nodded, his eyes on her even as he spoke. "Dad, pray. Please."

Sloane blinked back tears, reaching to hug first Shanley and then Shamus before she turned to her father, swept into his arms and held tight even as he prayed a powerful prayer for wisdom and protection. No one knew what was in the box, but they knew something was. It would change what they knew, they felt.

Carefully working at the lid, Shanley was finally able to pry it off, setting the box back down on the table, the lid laying loose on top. He looked around at the ones gathered before he looked at Sloane.

"Sloane? When it disappeared, what did you have it in?"

She looked up at him, startled. "Nothing. It was empty. I was going to use it for jewelry but hadn't got that far as Mom and Dad gave me that jewelry chest for my birthday that year."

Shanley nodded. "That's what I thought. There is something in there. I can feel it moving. I'm not sure what though." He looked up as Reilly handed Shamus a camera. "Right. Good idea. Shamus, start your magic before I move the lid."

Shamus nodded, the camera raised, even as he pointed to a spot. "What's that? I don't remember any writing on it."

"There wasn't." Sloane frowned. "Are we sure this is my box?"

Chapter 22

Her two brothers stared at her as they took in her words.

"I thought you recognized it?" Shanley struggled to understand what she was saying.

"I thought I did. But maybe it's not mine."

"Shanley, turn it over."

Shanley stared at Shamus for a moment and then did that, his heart sinking as he saw the engraving. "It's yours, Sloane. Gramps put your name on it before he gave it to you."

She nodded, her body shaking with fear. "Take the lid off, Shamus. Please?"

He watched her intently before moving aside for Redmond to gather his bride close to him. "You're sure, Sloane?"

"I am. This may be the answer that we need."

Shamus moved the lid, the camera back up to take photos, before he turned to her. "Sloane, when the box disappeared, did anything else?'

She stared at her brother, her brow wrinkling. "No. Just the box. Why?"

"Because there are stones in here. I suspect they are uncut jewels."

"Jewels?" Sloane stared at him before she turned to Redmond. "Where did they come from?"

"I have no idea, but we'll look into it." Redmond stared down at her even as she spoke. "Shamus, is there anything else in there?"

"No, just the jewels."

"Then, we're out of here. Sloane needs to get away. Dad, we'll be in the apartment."

The men watched the couple walk away before turning back to the box. Reilly stepped away, his phone out, taking a call that had come in. He spun, his eyes on Shamus as he listened, before he pocketed his phone.

Shamus approached him. "Reilly?"

"Shamus, how much trouble are you in?"

"Trouble? Me? None that I know of. I don't have any active investigations on the go that would lead to that. Why?"

"Because Emma just called me. She's hearing rumours that you've had a contract put out on you."

Shamus shook his head. "Not me. I don't have that kind of clientele that would do that." He sighed even as he looked up. "But to get to Sloane, they'd do that, wouldn't they?"

"That's right. Now we have to keep you safe as well." Reilly sounded disgruntled, causing Shamus to grin at him. "This is not funny, Shamus."

"I know it's not, but it seems that this is par for the course, doesn't it? And who gets to tell Sloane."

Reilly tilted his head, looking behind Shamus. "I think you just did."

Shamus groaned. "She's behind me? Don't tell me that."

Sloane spoke, anger in her voice. "What did they threaten you with, Shamus? They put out a contract on you? When does this end?" She spun, seeking comfort from Redmond, whose face was dark with anger.

"Reilly?"

"Emma called. There's a contract out on Shamus."

"I know that.   She called us too. Where does this leave us?"

"Hiding for now." Sloane shoved at him, not able to make him release her. "Redmond?"

"No, you're not running. Not anymore. It's come time to start making some concrete plans."

"And just how do we do that?   We have no better idea who is after us than we did."

"No, we have a better idea." Riordan approached them. "I just got confirmation on Greene. He was involved in smuggling when he was younger. And it connects to us."

"Leah's place."

Riordan nodded. "That's correct, Reilly. Somehow, the smugglers twenty years ago came in on her shoreline, passed her house and then headed here. Greene was their contact to the black market."

"And then how does it tie in with that last extraction?"

"That? It was Greene who sent us in. That information has just been clarified"

Redmond stood, his arms tight around Sloane, even as he stared at his father, trying to take it all in. "But he's not the head, the leader?"

"No, he's not. He was a lower man on the pole, shall we say? We're working now to identify his contacts. And we will find them. I can guarantee you that." Riordan was angrier than he had been in years, knowing this affected not just his family but Sloane's as well. And to find the leader, they had a lot of work to do, and a lot of preparation to keep the young couple in front of him safe. He had no doubt they were in more danger than his other four children had been.

Chapter 23

Sloane stared down at the book she was trying to read, realizing she had read the same page over and over. She sighed, setting the book aside. She needed to be busy, to be doing something but she wasn't allowed to leave the building. She needed fresh air.

Redmond watched her from the kitchen doorway before he approached, her coat in his hand.

"Come on, sweetheart. We can go out into the covered yard. It should be safe enough."

"We can?" Sloane was on her feet, her jacket on, heading for her boots.

"You really don't want to go outside, do you?" Redmond laughed at the glare she sent his way. "I guess that you do. I should have thought of that sooner. Dad's cleared it with our guys. They'll be on guard, but outside the tall fence."

Sloane paced the yard, content to be in the outdoors. She didn't handle being stuck inside for long.

"Redmond?"

"Yes, sweetheart?"   He had been sitting on the picnic table, watching her pace.

"What are you going to do when this is all over?"

"Find an island and run away with my wife?"   He grinned at her as she shook her head.   "No, I think I'll stay working with Dad.   He's setting our business differently now.   He's heading towards being a link in the chain, setting up contacts with other companies who do what we do.   He also wants us to train them."

"That sounds fair."   She slid down beside him, her arm wrapped around his, her head against his shoulder.   "Is your family safe?"

"So far, I would say so. They're alert, as are yours." He grew quiet, knowing she had a reason for asking, but hadn't quite figured out how to do that.

"I worry about them. I don't want to see them hurt, not on my account. I understand Reilly is tracking down the jewels."

"He has been. They weren't stolen, as far as he can determine, but he has no idea how they ended up in that box of yours or in that tree."

"Was it the man we found?"

"No, I don't think so. The box has to have been taken by someone who knew you." He felt her tense. "You have a suspicion?

She sighed. "I do. Greene's daughter used to drop in on us. We never liked her. I found her one day coming down from our upstairs. She had no reason to be there. It was after that I found the box gone, but I couldn't accuse her. I didn't see her take it."

"No, you couldn't. Where would we find her?"

"You don't. She overdosed about four years ago." Sloane grew quiet again. "There were rumours that it wasn't an accident, and I tend to believe that. She hated drugs, alcohol, all that. I never saw her do anything outside of the law." She twisted her head to look up at him. "And now, I've just opened up another line of investigation, didn't I?"

Redmond shook his head. "Dad said they've already looked at her and cleared her. I didn't know it was the same girl. He only had the one daughter?"

"He did. And one son, Ryan. Now, Ryan I could see doing something like this, taking the box, filling and then hiding it. But I don't understand if he did, why he never retrieved it."

"Then, it couldn't have been him. Do you remember anyone else you didn't know around?"

She shrugged. "It's a tourist area. There were always strangers around, so I couldn't say if there was someone or not."

She grew quiet as did he. He finally roused, realizing they had been outside for quite a while and he was growing cold. He drew her back into the building, heading for the conference room to her surprise.

Chapter 24

Redmond stood for a moment, his eyes on the tree they had taken apart, before he moved towards it. He was out here on his own. He hadn't told anyone he was coming, although he suspected Sloane knew. He searched the cavity, a frown on his face as he felt something, pulling that something free and then tucking it into his jacket before he moved away, heading back for his car. He didn't see the man who stood watching, an angry look on his face before he followed Redmond, not in time to prevent him from leaving.

Redmond shrugged out of his jacket, dropping it onto a chair in the conference room, his hands already working to undo the oilcloth package. He carefully removed it, studying the papers in front of him before he unfolded them, fear once more clenching at his heart. He was on the move, looking for his father, the papers in his hands.

"Dad? Have a moment?"

Riordan looked up as Redmond appeared in his doorway. "I do, son, always for you. What do you have there?"

"I was back out to the tree and found this package. Covered in oilcloth. These papers were in it. I don't like them, Dad."

"And why not?"

"Because it's an account of Greene and his cronies. It gives names, dates, amounts, what they stole, what they smuggled, who it came from."

"An accounting? And who put it there?"

"I don't know and I wish I did. I wonder if it was one of the men, put there for security purposes, and then they couldn't retrieve it."

"That's more than likely what happened. But there's something more?"

Redmond nodded. "It's just not an accounting of their activities. It's a list of men they want to destroy or kill. William, Shamus and Shanley are on the list. And I don't think they know that or why."

"I doubt that they do. Where's Sloane?"

"With Mom. They said something about it getting close to Christmas and needing to do some baking."

"Good. That will keep them occupied for a while. Where's Reilly?"

"He and Aideen took off yesterday for a couple of days. He said you were fine with that."

"That's right. I had forgotten. Then it's just you and I."

"I would suggest we email these to Rory, Regan and Ryanne. They can work on it as well."

Riordan reached for the papers. "I would rather not send this out anywhere, not until we know what or who we're facing."

Redmond stared at him. "You don't suspect one of our men, do you?"

Riordan shook his head. "No, not really, but someone is watching us too closely. They are trying to get to you two."

"I know. Sloane's starting to get cabin fever and I must say, so am I. I want this over, Dad. I want to be able to take her out for a meal, for a walk, away for a weekend, and not have to look over our shoulders."

"It will come, son. This is what the others went through, remember?"

"I remember. It doesn't make is any easier, you know?"

Riordan laughed at that, even as his eyes dropped to the papers. "This is very interesting. I know some of these men. I would never have suspected that they would be involved in anything like this."

"So, what all are we looking at? Not just robbery?"

Riordan sat back, his eyes on his son, judging how much he could tell him. "No, it's not. I must be frank with you, Redmond. I have been researching some of these names, not knowing this would show up. I'm finding that they are being blackmailed. Some have been forced into thefts, to fraud, to money laundering. Some have died because they refused. This is a vicious group that we're looking for."

Redmond had paled at his father's words. "So, the man from Alberta? He was part of it, after all?"

Riordan finally nodded. "I would think so. I have spoken with his wife. She said he was involved in something he refused to tell her about and came this way to investigate it. All he said was that he had been approached to become part of a conglomerate and didn't feel comfortable with some of the men involved."

"And they killed him."

Riordan shook his head. "No, it was his heart. I confirmed with his wife that he did have a heart condition. She hadn't wanted him to travel. How this was all covered up? I suspect we'll find out as we're working through all this." His gaze dropped back to the papers and he didn't hear Redmond give an exclamation and then rise, heading to find his bride.

Redmond stood for a moment in the kitchen doorway of the apartment, listening to his mother and Sloane talking and then realizing Anna was there as well. I am glad both mothers are here, he thought. Sloane needs that.

Sloane looked up at that point, a smile on her face as she saw him. "Come for samples, have you?"

"If there are some."

"Nope, none. We made sure of that." She giggled as his arms swept around her and he picked up one of the cookies she had just taken off the cookie sheet.

"These are good. Anna, I'm glad you are here. I need to ask both you and Sloane something."

"I don't like the sounds of that." Sloane turned her head and took a bite from his cookie, causing Redmond to grumble in pretended outrage and the two mothers to exchange an amused look.

"No, it's not that bad. Christmas is coming up. I pray this is all over by then. But where and how do we celebrate?"

They just shook their heads at him and sent him on his way. He paused in the doorway, looking back at Sloane, sudden fear for her safety and life running through him. He knew it was far from over and that they had just begun to enter the centre of their storm. Lord, protect my lady, please?

Keep her safe. Bring her through safely to
the other side.

Chapter 25

Rory watched for a moment as Redmond and their mother sorted through the training material they had complied, stacking the piles neatly before they stopped, deep in conversation. He was worried about his oldest brother, not quite sure why. He turned away, finding Sloane standing behind him, a question on her face.

"Rory? You're here."

"I am. Listen, do you have a couple of minutes?"

She nodded. "This sounds serious."

"No, it's not. Not really. I just need to ask you something." He pointed to the office he usually used when there. "Sit, please."

She watched as he moved papers and pens around his desk before she sighed. "Moving stuff isn't asking the questions you want to ask."

Rory shook his finger at her. "Behave yourself. But you're right. It doesn't." He sat back, watching her closely. "Dad mentioned that some of the men they're investigating smuggled stuff through Leah's property. Have you ever had any inkling of smuggling going on around here, given how close you are to the lake?"

She shrugged. "There are lots of stories about it. People have been named. Investigations have been done. But nothing has ever been proven. They say smuggled goods have come ashore near here." She looked down for a moment, concentrating on her thoughts. "I can't say that I've ever really paid much attention to this." She looked up at him. "Shamus would be the one to talk to. Dad, maybe he's heard something. That I can't say. Shanley was too wrapped up in his studies even as a teenager to pay much attention to gossip."

"I have a call into Shamus but haven't heard back from him." Rory watched her closely as she shrugged.

"If he's deep into an investigation, he won't answer. He'll let it go to voice mail and then clear the backlog at some point.

Dad? He's around but I'm not sure where. Shanley's away at a conference until next week."

Rory nodded, his eye still on her. "And how are you coping, Sloane? I understand that it's not easy. Leah told me that on numerous occasions. She's worried about you."

Sloane just shrugged. "I don't know how I'm doing. I just get through each day, the same as Redmond does." She rose, her eyes on the doorway. "I can't help you, Rory. It's not that I don't want to, it's that I can't. I don't know what you want to know. Everyone keeps asking me about things and I have no idea what or who or even where." She walked away with that, leaving him staring after her, suspicious that she knew something.

Redmond watched Sloane for a moment and then turned to Rory. "Rory?"

"Redmond? I thought you and Mom were busy."

"We were." Redmond sat in the chair that Sloane had just vacated. "What was that with Sloane?"

"We're digging into information, Redmond. We're tracking smuggling from Leah's place. William had mentioned at some point smuggling near here. I just asked if she knew of it. She says no."

"But you think she does and has forgotten?"

Rory shook his head. "No. I think if she knew, she'd tell us. She wouldn't hide anything like that. She wants this over, just like you do, and like the rest of us do for you."

Redmond sat, deep in thought, his brother's eyes on him, before he finally shook his head. "I don't know, Rory. I can see it happening, but there has been nothing definite to say it did. Dad said he's at a dead end with that investigation, unless something happens to start it up again."

Rory nodded. "There is a piece of information out there that will solve this. A person we need to find."

Redmond agreed, sighing as he shifted to pull out his phone. "This thing has not stopped all day. Hang ups. Unknown numbers." He glared at the phone before he swiped and pulled up his text messages. "It's from Regan. She and Delaney are on their way here. Now why?"

Rory shrugged. "I have no idea. She mentioned she needed to talk to Mom about something when I talked to her earlier." He grinned. "She'll corner you, you know. Pick your brain. Find out what all you don't know about what it is going."

Redmond began to laugh. Rory had described Regan so well. "She will. Now, where can we head off to where we won't have to go through one of her interrogations?"

"She'll track you down." He looked up. "Sloane?"

Redmond was on his feet, his hands on Sloane's upper arms. "Sloane? What it is?"

"Lad. He's been hurt." She thrust her phone at him. "Dad found him. He's on the way to the vet's with him. He's not sure what all is wrong with him."

Redmond tossed her phone to Rory, wrapping her into his arms, sitting back down, his eyes closed in prayer. He could feel her shudders as she fought back her sobs and could hear Rory as he talked to William.

Redmond finally looked at Rory, who sat, eyes focused on Sloane's phone before he looked up.

"Rory? How bad?"

"He's been poisoned, William thinks. The vet is optimistic. He doesn't think he ingested enough poison to kill him. They'll monitor him over the next few hours. Sloane, do you want to go there?"

She looked, a strained look on her white face. "That's what they want, isn't it? They want me to go there, and that's when I'll disappear, won't I?"

"More than likely. It's a ploy to get you and Redmond out into the open. They're getting desperate. They need to get to you two and they can't while you're in here. Unfortunately, at some point, you will leave here and that's what we need to watch out for." He looked up as Riordan appeared in the doorway, his eyes on Redmond and Sloane. "Dad?"

"I just heard. Sloane, if you want to be there, we'll get you there."

She sighed, her head going down against Redmond. "No. I'll wait. It's better if I'm not there. He won't let them treat him if I am and he knows I'm upset. That's the bond we have."

Riordan nodded before motioning for Rory to go with him. Redmond sat, his arms tight around Sloane, his head resting against hers, his heart breaking for her. He prayed, not sure what he was praying, but knowing that God understood.

Chapter 26

Sloane was on a mission a few days later. She headed for the conference room, walking around the table, searching the material, before she sighed, her eyes raised to the walls. She ran for the supply room, finding rolls of papers, markers, pens, highlighters and sticky notes in many colours. She needed to visualize all that material, she thought, and the computer just didn't work for that. She reached for tape as well, heading back to the conference room, not seeing Regan watching her before she followed Sloane.

Regan watched for a moment before she moved to help, not saying a word, just working in silence with Sloane to post paper on the wall, before she reached for a stack of notes.

"How do you want this on there, Sloane?"

"Names, first. Dates. Locations. Deaths. Material found. Whatever we can find. A separate sheet for each I think."

"Good. If we run out of room here, we take over another room."

The two women worked away, quiet words between them as necessary, before Regan stepped back for a moment, rubbing at her neck, her eyes searching their papers.

"This is good, Sloane. Is this how you would do a search?"

"Not really. This is how I used to lay out my notes for a paper. I would put each idea on a separate paper and then combine them." She stood beside Regan, content to be with Redmond's sister for the moment. "How did you do it? How did you cope?"

"Prayer. Delaney and I talked a lot. It was tough. As you can tell, my voice will never be the same. At the beginning, I could barely talk.   Until we found out the medication I was taking affected that."

Redmond and Delaney watched the two women before they exchanged glances, Delaney's look amused.   Redmond just shook his head before he walked up, wrapping Sloane in a hug, causing a small squeak to come from her.   Regan leaned against her husband, not looking at him, her eyes on a paper, before she walked over, her fingers tracing the writing.

"Sloane? What were we trying to decide with this one?"

Sloane shrugged. "I have no idea, Regan. I think we were just putting down any and all thoughts and ideas that came to mind with each lead there."

Redmond read the paper. "Who are those people? The Aldersons?"

"The Aldersons are one of the oldest families in town. Their ancestors had a flour mill before they gave that up and strictly ran a store in town. The hardware store is run by one of their descendants. Why?"

"Why? Because that's not a name I remember us looking at." They all turned as they heard Riordan respond to the question.

Sloane shook her head. "I'm not sure that we should but the name did show up." She leaned against Redmond, her hand on her cheek, eyes thoughtful. "I would suggest you talk to Dad about them. I'm not sure on their history, other than what I said."

"We will do that." Riordan walked slowly around the room, stopping to reach

each paper. "You two ladies did good. This is so visual, we can track from one paper to another as we need to." He turned his eyes first on the two ladies and then raising to the two younger men. He sighed. Redmond has dragged Regan into this, against Delaney's wishes. He'll support her, but I know he's not real happy about it.

"Dad? Where does the investigation stand with the police?" Redmond's quiet voice finally broke through the stillness in the room.

"Not where it should be. The investigator said it's gone cold. They don't have any new information that would lead them to anyone or anywhere in fact."

"In other words, we're basically on our own." Redmond sighed. "This is not what I wanted to hear."

"I know, son. It's not what any of us want to hear. Sloane, your brother has been working on it as he can. He's funnelling information to us as he can."

"I knew he would be. He won't let it rest until he solves it." She grinned. "You know it will become a race between you and he to do just that."

Riordan grinned at her suddenly, looking like his oldest son for a moment. "And which one of us will win?"

"Regan and I. We'll just keep plugging away at this and we'll solve it." Sloane moved away from Redmond, her eyes on one of the papers. "This house. It's been vacant for years, but I know the police have been there on many occasions." She spun, her eyes on Redmond. "We need to take a look at it."

"No, we do not. Dad and Reilly will go. You're not going out somewhere like that. It's out in the country, isn't it?"

She nodded. "It is. The brush has grown close to it. The fire department has been after the absentee owner to clear it up."

"Absentee owner? Who is that?" Riordan had been listening closely to her words.

She turned back to her pages and then pointed. "Them. The Evans. And they are related to the Aldersons. Cousins, I believe."

"So, it comes back to the Aldersons."
Riordan looked up. "Reilly! Just who I
needed. There are some names you need to
research for me."

"In a minute, Dad." He held up an
envelope. "This just came for Sloane."

Sloane walked slowly across the room,
her hand out for the envelope, sudden fear in
her heart. "Does it say who it came from?"

Reilly shook his head. "No. Just your
name written on it. Somehow it ended up in
the mail."

Sloane slowly opened the envelope,
then sighed. "It's okay. It's from Shamus."
She handed the letter to Redmond. "Here.
He's found information on the Aldersons."

Chapter 27

Redmond paused on the sidewalk outside a store later that week, his eyes searching the window displays before he looked over at his father. Riordan stood, his back to the store, watching the traffic, the pedestrians, and then the stores across the street. The two men had come to Sloane's hometown for the day, not telling her. Redmond regretted that, but he knew she would have insisted on coming if she had been told. Right now, they needed to come in as strangers, if possible, not as someone connected to the town.

Redmond reached for the handle of the door, feeling the weight of the old wooden door as he pulled it open. He stepped inside, hearing his father's footsteps right behind him, and then moved to one side, his eyes wide for a moment as he took in the store.

Riordan moved slowly through the store, assessing the people who were shopping, the store staff, looking for an owner and not finding one. He finally approached the man he was told was the manager and put in a request to speak with the owner.

The manager had simply shaken his head, stated the owners were never on site, that they had other interests they were involved with and any paperwork was simply left of a desk in their office, and he would come in the next day and find it completed and on his desk. He never saw them.

Riordan thanked the man, and slowly walked back through the store, exiting and then walking through nearby stores, just observing. He finally turned as Redmond approached.

"What now, Dad?"

"Home, I think, Redmond. The owners were in the hardware store. I spoken with different store owners. They all have ideas of what those people are up to, but won't commit to anything. I think we need to send in someone undercover for a few day."

Redmond nodded, even as he slipped into his father's car and reached for his seatbelt. "We may need to. Let's talk to Sloane's people first."

"I agree. They're coming for dinner tonight, your mother said. She had asked them before this all came up."

"All of them?" At Riordan's nod, Redmond smiled. "Good. Sloane needs her family. Now, about her dog?"

"Lad? Yes, we'll bring him in. They need each other."

"Good." Redmond didn't realize he was repeating himself, his thoughts already on his observations from that morning. "That hardware store, Dad? It seems busy, but it doesn't seem to be moving a lot of material or supplies."

"That's my impression. The owners are absentee. The manager said they had other projects they are involved in."

"I don't like that, Dad. They should be around the store and aren't."

Redmond walked slowly towards his office, his mind on their observations from the morning, looking up to see Sloane standing in front of him. He reached to hug her, finding her shaking.

"Sloane?" When she didn't respond, he swept her into a chair in his office, crouching down beside her, an arm around her. "Sweetheart?"

"Mom called. They're on their way here. They had a fire in their back shed early this morning. She told me there was a warning note on their front door, that whoever it was wants me."

"I'm sure they do. But why? That's what we don't know."

She nodded, sudden fatigue on her face. "Where were you, Redmond?"

"Dad and I? We took a stroll through your town this morning, looking for answers."

"And not finding them, I suppose." She sighed, sitting back in the chair, rubbing at her face. "The Aldersons are never in the hardware store. The other store owners would be too scared to talk. There have been rumours, which we all discounted, of payments being forced from the store owners. Fingers have pointed at the hardware store."

"That's what we wondered. No proof? Protection money?"

"That's what Dad says. He's never been approached. Apparently it's rumoured just to be the few stores around the hardware. If a store shuts down or moves, they don't pay."

Redmond rose, pacing, before he stopped, his eyes on his desk and the papers tidily piled on it. "So, where do we do, Sloane? Do you have any idea?"

She nodded and spoke a name, her eyes on her husband as he looked at her, shock on his face at first before he nodded.

"That makes sick sense, you know. Tell me what you know about him."

"We can't say anything to my family, Redmond. Not a thing. They trust him."

"I get that, sweetheart. I'll work it for now."

"That friend of yours?"

"Emma? You want her involved?"

"We need someone not directly connected to us to search. That way, we can say we didn't look into it. I know the people. They'll claim a setup if we do."

"I'll call Emma for you. Here." He stood, walked around the desk and just swept her into his arms, returning to sit in his chair.

Shocked, Sloane stared at him before she shook a finger. "You need to stop this, Redmond."

"Nope. I like holding my wife." He simply grinned at her before he reached for his phone. "So, let's call Emma."

Before he had a chance to dial, his phone chimed. Sloane leaned over to look at the number. "Emma? How'd she do that?"

Redmond had trouble controlling his laughter as he answered the phone. "Emma? I was just about to call you. Sloane wants to know how you knew to call."

"She did?" Emma sounded distracted for a moment. "Isaac. No. Don't touch the pens. There are your crayons." She came back on the line. "Sorry. I'm working from home and Isaac wants attention." She was referring to Abe's and hers young son.

"That's okay. Why were you calling?" Redmond watched Sloane's face, a frown on his for a moment.

"I called you, didn't I? Now, why?"

Redmond began to laugh. "That's what I just asked you, Emma."

He heard a huff from her and then she began to speak rapidly, even as he scrambled to take notes.

"I'll send you my findings, Redmond. I'm still working through some of the names."

"I'm sure you are. We had one of those names. Thanks for the information."

Sloane leaned forward to read the names before she stood and paced, her face white. "This is getting worse and worse, Redmond. How do we stop it?"

"We don't. We need to work it through. That's the only way you and your family will be safe."

"But how safe are we? Really? I mean right now. How safe are we?"

Redmond shook his head, knowing he didn't have an answer for her and that she really didn't expect one.

Chapter 28

Shamus watched his sister closely that night, alarmed at how much weight she had lost and the whiteness of her face. He turned to Redmond, studying him as well.

"Redmond?"

Redmond shook his head. "I know, Shamus. I've had her out in the yard, but it's not the same. This is really beginning to weigh heavily on her, on us all. I don't know what to say."

Shamus nodded. "We need to solve this and solve this now. How do we do just that?"

Redmond shrugged, his attention turning to Shanley for a moment. "What's going on with Shanley?"

"What do you mean?" Shamus spun to study his brother, not seeing anything odd about him.

"He's hiding something, Shamus." Redmond walked towards Shanley, a hand on his arm drawing him to one side. "Shanley?"

Shanley shook his head. "I don't know, Redmond. You're asking me what's wrong, aren't you? I just feel such a sense of doom and danger. I can't pinpoint where or who."

"That's what we're picking up as well." Shamus stood shoulder to shoulder with his brother, his eyes on Redmond. "Where do we stand?"

Redmond sighed to himself. "We're almost at a dead end, I think. We have worked and traced everyone and everything as much as we can. Without new information, we just don't know where to look."

Shamus stared across the room as his sister as she and Regan teased Reilly and Rory. "She's fit in with your family, Redmond. She always said she would never marry. That she couldn't and wouldn't fit in with anyone else's family."

"I think she was saying that to protect herself and to protect her family."

Shanley lowered the glass of lemonade he had been to drink from. "And why would you say that?"

"Because she has felt threatened for years. She has known her family has been threatened for years. She's just opening up to me about that. She'll talk to me in the dead of the night, when it's dark. She has felt fear since before she found that body, Shamus. She can't pinpoint who or why. We're working through that." He didn't tell the other two men that he held his wife as she sobbed and shook with terror as she spoke, that all he could do was pray for her until she relaxed enough to fall asleep in his arms, leaving him to lie awake and worry and fret before he too slept.

Shanley stared at his sister. "She has never said. I know she did change after that incident. But you say it's been going on since before then?"

Redmond nodded. "She says it has. I have no reason to doubt her word."

"Shanley, back off Redmond." Shamus shook his head at his brother. "We know how closed she can be when she wants to be. She would not have said anything if she feared for us or Mom and Dad.”

“That fire this morning?” Redmond changed the subject, not wanting to be caught in an argument betweeen the brothers.

“Yeah, that fire.” Shamus leaned back against a wall. “Dad tried to go and put it out. Mom wouldn’t let him out of the house. Lad just about went crazy.”

“They were likely waiting for one of them to come out. They would have used them against Sloane.”

“They would have.” Shamus was adamant on that. “I just don’t get why.”

Chapter 29

Redmond stepped away from the conference room, his emotions roiling. He had spoken with Emma just a few moments prior, only to hear that Abe and his men were on their way towards them. Emma had received word that things were heating up towards Sloane and Abe felt it necessary to step in, at least for a bit. Redmond wasn't quite sure how he felt. He knew, he thought, how Sloane would feel. He turned, leading against the wall opposite the doorway, watching her as she moved around the room, stopping every once in a while to stare at a paper, or to add a name or detail. He knew the moment she realized who it was and watched as she crumpled to the floor, his feet already sending him in motion as he called for his father and Reilly.

He simply swept her into his arms as he dropped to the floor, feeling her stiffness and then tilting his head to watch her face.

"You figured out who?"

She nodded. "I have. And it's not who I thought. How could they? How could they do that to our town, to our people?"

Riordan dropped to a crouch beside her, his hand on her shoulder, even as Reilly stared at the paper she had just marked, shock on his face.

"Sloane? What happened?"

"That." Her finger trembled as she pointed. "Him. And her. How could they?"

Riordan spun slightly to stare behind him, watching as Reilly traced the name, before he gave a grim nod. "That's who I've been narrowing down my search to. Now, how do we keep you safe?"

She snorted. "That won't happen. He's got too many friends around here and his fingers are into many pies, as Mom would say."

"Abe." Redmond's single word, softly spoken, caught the attention of the other three.

"No, he can't!" Sloane groaned. "I don't want him here."

Redmond looked over her head as he heard footsteps. "I'm sorry, Sloane. He's here. I just heard from Emma before you saw the name. If I could have stopped him, I would have."

Sloane shoved away from him, her running feet taking her past the men, who stared after her before entering the conference room, to face Redmond's devastated look and the grim looks on Riordan and Reilly's faces.

"Redmond?" Abe's quiet question finally broke through the silence.

"She knows, Abe. She knows who it is. And I'm afraid she'll go out and confront him or her."

"We need to keep her from doing just that." Abe turned to his men, after a nod from Riordan, and sent them around the building.

"I hope you're not too late. She may already have escaped." Redmond headed for the apartment, fear in his heart that she had done just that. He found her crumpled on the floor just inside the door, sobs shaking her body. He swept her into his arms, carrying her to the chair he favoured and just sat, holding her, his heart breaking for her.

"Redmond?"

"Ssh, sweetheart. We'll figure it out."

"But it may be too late by that time. How do we stop them?"

"Abe's here. He'll work on that with Dad and Reilly. Shamus will want to be involved, we know that."

"And Dad. And Shanley." She reached for Lad as he stood, his nose poking at her. "How do we keep everyone safe?"

"I have no idea. We'll work on it."

She shoved at him but he didn't release her. "You keep saying that. How?"

Chapter 30

Two weeks had passed. Abe and his men had headed home after that first day, Abe giving advice, his men working with Riordan's sons and his men to ensure that there was as much security around the couple as they could put. Sloane chafed at the restrictions, not used to them. Redmond worried about her, even as he worked with his family in the new training company they had set up. He knew Sloane would not take many more restrictions and he tried to think of a way to ease it for her.

He finally approached her, his hands finding hers and drawing her to the outside, to the yard they had claimed as theirs.

"Sloane, we need to do something."

She nodded. "We do. I can't live like this, Redmond. You need to be back at your home. I need freedom to move around."

"I know. We're moving home tonight. We need to. And starting tomorrow, we'll be out and about. I don't want you out on your own. I would like it if someone is with you, but you need your freedom back."

She nodded again, reaching to hug him. "No one will like this."

"I know, but we have to. If we stay hidden, we won't find the men or women responsible for your terror."

"No, we won't. I want this over, Redmond, and just how do we do that? They've taken days from us that we'll never get back."

"I know. How about we dress up tonight and go out for a meal?"

Her eyes shone. "Do you mean that?"

"I do. Find your fanciest bib and tucker, Mrs. Stuart. Mr. Stuart is asking for the pleasure of your company for a meal on the town."

She hugged him harder, her tears wetting his cheek where her face touched his before she was up, running for the bedroom. He could hear the opening and closing of drawers and knew she was packing for them.

He stood, his fingers rubbing together before he headed to find his car. He needed to ensure it was in good running condition.

Late that afternoon, Riordan stared at the open apartment door before he entered, not quite sure what he would find. Reilly stood just inside the door, arms crossed, a grin on his face.

"They made a break for it, did they, Dad?"

"It looks as if they have. I would say they've headed home." He reached for his phone as it chimed, a sigh rising from him. "It's your brother."

"Which one? I have two, and two brothers-in-law."

"Redmond." He stared at the phone for a moment, not quite sure how he wanted to respond. "Redmond?"

"Dad? You're in the apartment, aren't you?"

"I am and so is Reilly, who by the way thinks this is amusing." Riordan watched as Reilly's grin grew larger and he heard Redmond laughing. "This is not funny, Redmond."

"I know, Dad, but I can just picture you two. You standing there all grim and upset, Reilly leaning against a wall, a grin on his face."

Riordan pulled his phone from his ear to stare at it, causing Reilly to break out into laughter. "You pegged us, son. Now, where are you?"

"We moved home, Dad. We needed this. Sloane needs her freedom. She needs her privacy as well. I know. I know. The apartment is private, but it's not the same as our home."

"You're right, son. I should have thought of that."

"Just wanted you to know. And I'm taking my wife out on a date tonight."

"You're what?" Riordan's voice rose in his surprise, finding that Redmond had ended the call. He stared at his phone once more before he heard Reilly saying something in an amused voice. "What did you say?"

"He hung up on you, didn't he? He's always wanted to do that, you know." Reilly tried to restrain his laughter without much success.

Riordan finally grinned. "He did and he has. Now, he says he's taking his wife out for a meal. Does that make sense?"

"It does, Dad. They're newlyweds, not having had the kind of freedom to do that. Send one of the men to search the restaurants in town, and when he finds them, he can watch from outside. That won't be intrusive on them."

Riordan nodded, finally agreed with Reilly. "I can do that. You're elected." He grinned at Reilly's protest.

Aideen finally tracked her husband down, her own eyes amused as she watched him pace their living room.

"Dad send you out on a job tonight, love?"

"He did. He's sending me out to track down Redmond and Sloane and then sit outside the restaurant to watch."

Aideen held up the bag she carried. "Then, it's a good thing I packed us a meal."

"Us? A meal?"

She nodded. "I'm going with you. You'll need company."

Reilly just laughed as he hugged her and then kissed her. "You are so right, my dear. Let's head out. I don't want to follow them, but I do need to start looking."

Reilly finally parked near his brother's car in the parking lot of a local fancy restaurant. Aideen nodded. "I thought this is where he would come."

Reilly stared at her. "You let me search all those other places."

She began to giggle, drawing his own smile. "Did you really think he would take her to a fast food place?"

He shrugged. "Not really, but I had to start somewhere."

They watched later as Redmond and Sloane walked towards them before Redmond tucked her into his car and then walked towards Reilly's vehicle.

"You pulled the short straw, did you?" Redmond leaned against the door for a moment.

"There were no straws to draw. Dad told me I had to."

Redmond grinned at Aideen as she laughed. "Thanks, Reilly. We're heading home. I suggest you two do the same."

Reilly shook his head. "We'll follow you and run interference if we need to."

Redmond sobered. "I pray it's not necessary."

"So do I, brother. So do I."

Chapter 31

Christmas Day came and went, with all the festivities and activities before and during that day. Redmond and Sloane had mingled and been present with their families but there was a hesitation there with them, that they felt they were putting their families in danger just by doing that. Redmond had just shaken his head whenever Sloane had asked if there was any news. She didn't like that there wasn't any, that whoever it was had seemed to stop. She sighed to herself finally, acknowledging that this was the pattern she had lived under for so many years. Except now, it was all out in the open and everyone was watching her, to assess if she had had news, to assess if she was coping. She had finally walked away from them all, finding a spot in the back of Redmond's yard, where she could curl up and not be noticed. Redmond knew where she was. He made sure to be around when she was outside, not crowding her, but letting her know he was there. She appreciated that.

She shivered one day as she sat, sorting through the mail, her hands reaching for the plain white envelope that had no name on it. She felt such a presence of evil and danger that she shoved her chair back, tumbling to the floor with it. Redmond heard the crash and was at the conference room door in seconds, on his knees beside her, his father behind him, two of their employees behind Riordan.

"Redmond?"

"I don't know, Dad. I heard the chair and ran."

"That envelope." Sloane rose to her feet, angry. "They're back. That envelope. Yes, that plain white one. It's from them." She stood, hands on her hips, staring at it. "This is how it always goes. They're quite over the holidays. I often suspected that they go away for a month or so, because it's always that long between threats."

The two men retreated, their eyes on Sloane before they exchanged a glance and a shrug. They had no idea what she was talking about.

Redmond paced the room, finally stopping beside her, his eyes on the letter. "You didn't open it."

"No. I won't. I haven't opened one of them in years."

"You haven't? Then how do you know it's from them?" Riordan reached for the letter

"I can feel the evil and hate from it." She threw up her hands. "And, of course, you don't believe me."

"No, we do. We've heard of this before." Riordan slid the paper from the envelope, his eyes on her before he unfolded it, a grim look crossing his face before he handed the letter to Redmond, his eyes finding Sloane.

"Dad?"

"Read it, Redmond. Then, we talk. Sloane, did you keep any of the letters?"

She shook her head. "No, I burned them. I prayed that they would stay away from me and my family. Now it looks as if I've brought my danger to you and your family."

"Not the first time we've been threatened." Riordan reached for the letter again, re-reading it. "It seems, Sloane, that your enemy and mine are related."

"They are? And does that mean Dad's is too?"

Riordan stared at her for a moment, before his eyes moved to Redmond. "I think they are. And I would hazard a guess that your trouble is related to your father. They couldn't get to him. They knew better than to try the boys. So, that left you or your mother. They chose you. The enemy that I have? Through all the trouble the other four went through, there was always something that didn't quite relate to what happened to them. It was directed at me."

"And it goes back to that last trip, doesn't it, Dad?"

"And what did they threaten, Riordan?" Sloane was not sure she really wanted to know.

"They're asking for the paperwork they say you have, which you don't. They are asking for the jewels, which you don't have. Those we turned over to the detective. They are asking to meet you, which we will not let them do." He looked around as Reilly approached, another envelope in his hand.

"Redmond? Those dinners you two have taken out? Your walks? The library? Church? Shopping? They have photos of them all." He held up the large envelope. "They are all in here."

Sloane stared at him before she shook her head. "I knew that would happen. It always does, doesn't it? At least on TV or in movies and books, it does."

"We knew this would happen as well, Sloane. That is why someone has been shadowing you."

She stared at Riordan before shaking her head again. "If you keep following us, they won't act."

"We don't want them too, sweetheart. We want to catch them before that happens." Redmond perched on the corner of a table, his eyes on her in a thoughtful manner. "What are you thinking?"

"I thinking I need to take an ad out in the local paper. Here and at home. Tell them to leave me alone. That I don't have what they want and never have had."

"That won't help, Sloane. It will make them angry and they'll come after you for sure." Reilly watched as she stiffened before she turned to him, anger flaring on her face.

"Maybe that's what I want."

"No, you don't. You want to keep Redmond and your family and our family safe. If you do that, you can't." Reilly watched as she fought it out inside her before she finally nodded.

"You're right, Reilly. I don't want anyone hurt." Her voice was so soft and sorrowful, they could barely hear her. "But how?"

"How?

"Yes, how. How do we stop them?"

"Now that we know what they want, I'll talk to the detective. He's been thinking of holding a news conference, updating the old case. That might make them back off."

"But you know they won't." Redmond spoke up, his eyes on his hands as he thought through the scenarios they could face. "I don't think they'll stop, Dad. Not the ones after you. It's been escalating all the time."

"It has had. I talked to William. He's been tracking incidents, not connecting them until now. He's talking to Shamus and Shanley as well to see what's been happening with them. I suspect the men in your life, Sloane, have not said anything, wanting to keep you and your mother safe."

She snorted, causing the men to grin. "And that has worked so well, now hasn't it?" She drew herself up on the table beside Redmond and leaned against him. "We need to come up with a plan. If you don't, I will."

"Not on your own, please, Sloane. Involve us." Riordan knew he was almost pleading. "And I know Abe wants to be part of it."

She just stared at the floor, her emotions in a mess, not sure where she wanted to be or to go. She didn't even feel as if God was listening to her. She had pleaded for so long for this to go away and it never had.

Chapter 32

Running for his front door, dodging the sleet hitting at him, Redmond unlocked it and then slid on the hardwood floor as he entered, seeing Sloane appear at the end of the hall.

"Sloane? You're here?"

"Of course, I am. I haven't been anywhere today. It's been too nasty. I dislike sleet." She walked into his hug.

"We got word that you had disappeared."

She leaned back to look up at him. "They're at it again, are they? It's been what, two weeks since the photos and that letter? It will continue every week for the next six weeks, and then it stops for about four or five weeks, and starts up again."

"They have a pattern?"

"They do. And if it's who we suspect, they always go away for that length of time, to somewhere hot, or so they say. I've often wondered if they just hid here somewhere.

Did you ever look for a home that's not in their name?"

"I think we did, but I'm not sure now." He reached for his phone, his hand hesitating as she shook her head.

"Tomorrow, Redmond. Or send off a text to Reilly and let him look tomorrow. Remember, we had plans for tonight, to go out, only the weather isn't cooperating."

He swung an arm around her as she turned to the kitchen. "But I can smell something very delicious. You've been concocting and cooking, as you say."

"I have been. Can you set the dining room table with the good dishes?"

"Are we celebrating?" He wasn't quite sure what she had in mind.

She stopped, hesitating before she turned back to him. "I know we made a pact that we would set aside one night a week as a date night, just to be together, not worrying about anything else. That should have been tonight. I just thought, with the weather so bad, we could do that here, dress up, use the good China." She turned away, her shoulders drooping. "I guess I should have asked you first."

Redmond sighed, his heart breaking for his bride, even as he prayed for her, knowing she was so stressed and having a difficult time really believing it would be over. He reached to hug her, drawing her back against him. "I think it's a wonderful idea. I think we need to get all dressed up. Can you wear that soft yellow dress?"

She turned her head, wonder on her face. "The long one? The velvet one?"

"That one. I love you in it. Now, what do we need to do right now?"

"Everything's cooking. We'll have time to change before it's ready." She spun in his arms, hugging him. "Thank you, my love."

He didn't tell her how scared he had been, when word had reached him. His father had just stared at him as he threw the letter at him and ran from the building. He didn't hear the men calling for him to wait. He drew out his phone, sending a quick text off to his father. His face grew grim even as he reached for his tuxedo, knowing that's what Sloane would not expect. He dressed, even as his mind raced through scenarios and plans and plots without deciding on a particular one.

Two days later, he approached his home, seeing the open door and the patrol vehicles parked haphazardly in front. He tried to make his way past them, but an officer held him back, shaking his head at his questions.

"I'm sorry, Redmond. I'm not sure what's going on. The security company called us, asking us to do a welfare check here."

Redmond slumped back against the hood of the patrol vehicle, not hearing his father's voice beside him. He waited, not sure if Sloane was there, if she was alive, hurt, missing.

He finally looked up as the detective approached.

"Evan?"

"She's not there, Redmond. Did she have plans to be anywhere today that you know of?" Evan Richards watched Redmond closely.

Redmond shook his head. "No, she didn't. She said she planned on staying home, working on some of the old reports her father's company is converting to digital." He looked past Evan at the house, his heart sinking. "She's not there?"

"I'm sorry, Redmond. She's not. The door was broken in, the locks smashed. I can't say if she was there or not. There doesn't seem to be much of a disturbance."

"She would have put up a fight, if she could have. That much I know." He sank back further on the car, slumping over, his arms wrapping around himself. "Where is she?"

"I have the crime scene team coming in. We'll find her for you."

"And will she be alive when you do? That's the million dollar question." Redmond shoved past his family, heading for his car, sitting in it for a moment, not stirring as he heard the door open and felt the car shift as someone sat in the passenger seat.

"You're not on your own, Redmond." Shamus' voice was tight and Redmond could hear the anger and the worry in it. "I'm sticking with you until we find her."

"And you're sure we will?"

Shamus nodded. "I am sure. God has told me that."

Redmond finally keyed the motor to life, but didn't drive away. "Where do we begin to look, Shamus? Do you have any idea?"

"I do. I've been looking into that name. Sloane wouldn't tell me, but I guessed. She didn't deny it when I directly asked her."

"No, she wouldn't. She wants proof."

"And we will find it." Shamus reached into his pocket, pulling out a piece of paper. "This is where we need to be. It's between our town and yours."

The two men huddled in their jackets, their breath visible in the cold night air, as they watched the house, seeing lights on and vehicles moving in and out from it.

"You're sure this is the right place?"

"I am." Shamus shifted on his feet, his eyes following the movement of the men walking the perimeter. "I'm just not sure if this is where they would bring her or not. We'll have trouble getting in to find out."

"I know. Ryanne went through something like this. We had to wait until most of the men left before Shea and I could move in."

"I pray we have time to wait." Shamus' attention was drawn to a van that had just pulled in. "Well, well. Look who's here."

Redmond's attention followed Shamus' gaze. "Wait! I know her. The detective's sister?"

"It looks like her. How certain are you on the detective?"

Redmond shrugged. "I have no idea. I thought he was clear but now? I don't know. We'll need to talk to our fathers and see what they have to say."

"And that we'll do later." Shamus' hand drew Redmond away from where they had been standing and through the brush to the back of the lot. "Here, I think we can move in from here."

"Are you sure?"

Shamus gave a quick grin. "No, not at all. But they don't seem to have people back here. If we can get close, we might be able to hear what's going on. It appears there are windows open."

Redmond stared at the house. "There are. That's so bizarre. Who has windows open like that in the wintertime?"

"Crazy people, that's who. I think it's to help clear out the inside. If they're drinking and smoking, they want that evidence to dissipate quickly, and there's no better way than open windows." He paused, pointing suddenly to the basement. "There

are lights on down there. I wonder why."
He moved forward quickly and quietly for
his height, Redmond on silent feet behind
him.

The two men paused, hanging tight to
the building, their eyes watchful before
Shamus bent to look through
the basement window. He rose, shaking his
head. "Nothing there."

They froze in place, faces buried as
best they could, as the back door opened and
two men appeared.

They listened to their conversation
before Redmond's hand gripped Shamus'
arm. He knew them. He also knew the
property they were speaking of. Sloane was
not at this location, he thought. Of course,
she wouldn't be. They would hide her, hide
her in plain sight. That only made sense.
They waited for the men to disappear before
they quietly moved away, heading for
Redmond's car.

"Redmond? What was that all
about?"

"She won't be there. I know the men.
They're talking about another property. One

on the other side of my town. They've taken Sloane there. We need to move and move quickly."

Shamus just shook his head, not sure what Redmond was up to, but willing to go along with him, if it meant finding his sister.

They stood once more in the shadows, Redmond's brow furrowed, as he watched the house. He prayed this was where she was. But he had no guarantees of that. Shamus tapped his shoulder, pointing to himself and then around the house. Redmond nodded, pointing to the opposite side. The men moved forward, feet carefully placed so as not to make a sound.

Redmond stood by the back door, his hand on the knob, hesitating before he moved away, his eyes searching the lighted windows. He finally paused by one, seeing it open, and stood close, his eyes on the light even as he moved closer, his ears straining to catch the conversation.

He finally nodded. He had been correct. Sloane was here. Now they had to find a way to get in and get her out without being found. He didn't hear the sounds of steps behind him before a hard object connected with the back of his head, driving him to his knees and then the ground. He was rolled over, searched and then dragged by his arms towards the back door, his head flopping limply with every movement of his body.

Shamus stood, shock on his face for a moment, before he moved towards the two men, hoping to reach them before Redmond disappeared into the house. He too never heard the sounds behind him until he was on his hands and knees from a blow from behind, then pulled to his feet, an arm around his neck choking him into submission. He was thrust forward down the basement stairs, his hand barely catching at the railing to help him keep his balance. He shook his head as he spun, then stopped, hands raising in the air at the weapon pointed at him. He backed up until he stood against the wall, his eyes not moving from the man, seeing Redmond dropped in a heap on the floor near him, not moving. He could hear soft sounds from near him and prayed that it was Sloane, but he didn't move his eyes, not until he was spun and then thrust towards one of the metal support posts and then shoved down, his hands bound behind him.

He blinked as the light was suddenly extinguished but not before he saw Redmond also bound to a support post. He caught a quick glimpse of a female form and prayed it was Sloane but he wasn't even sure of that, the glimpse had been too brief. His head went back as his eyes closed. This had not been their plan, not at all. He had no idea how badly hurt Redmond was. His eyes closed as he prayed, not knowing what was coming.

Chapter 34

Riordan walked through Redmond's house, finally allowed in, not seeing anything that would alarm him, and that worried him.   He knew Sloane had been home. He had talked to her earlier that day and she had told him she was planning on staying in.   He turned as he heard Reilly's voice and then Rory's.

Rory stood for a moment, his eyes on his father, before he turned, heading for the back door and then the outdoors, a powerful flashlight in his hand.   Reilly stood for a moment before he headed to the office, his eyes on the scattered papers on the floor. He frowned. This was not like Sloane. So, this must have been where she had been when she was taken. And that she was taken, none of them had any doubt. It was just unknown who.   And they knew there were two different parties involved, both after Sloane, but one after Redmond as well.   Reilly prayed for both his brother and his wife, knowing that was all he could do at the moment.

Riordan stood in the office doorway, his eyes on the papers, before he looked up and then around, heading for the book shelves, something there drawing his attention. He reached for the picture sitting there, his heart sinking. He knew who had his son's wife.   He just prayed both Redmond and Shamus were safe.

Reilly approached, his eyes on the photo, before they raised to his father.

"Dad?"

"Reilly, I know who has her. I just need to prove it."

"And that's going to be difficult. I can tell by the look on your face."

"It will be. Find Rory. We need to call the girls. And then we need to call that Emma."

"I already did, Dad. But you have a name to give her, don't you?"

"I do.   It's not one that I ever suspected. But I think Sloane and Redmond were heading that way with their investigation. I know they were working on their own."

"They were, Dad." Reilly held out a pad of paper. "I found this among the papers. Sloane had time to jot down a name before she disappeared. How she managed that, I would like to know."

"We'll ask her when we get her home."

"And you're sure that we will?"

"I am, Reilly. Just pray that she's not hurt bad." He looked down at the paper. "Have you heard from Redmond?"

"No. He and Shamus took off and haven't called in. Shanley called. I told him what happened. He was heading for their parents."

"If they will, have them come to the office. We need to start planning."

Rory walked back in at that point. "I just talked to Emma. She knew something had happened. She was to have a conference call with Sloane this afternoon around three. That never happened."

"And Redmond said he talked to her about two. That narrows down the time she disappeared."

"That's about when the security company put in their call."

"Rory?   Did Emma say much?" Riordan looked at his son, hoping that there was news.

"She has some news, Dad.   She had some more research she was waiting on and that she'd call later tonight.   She'll try you and then either Reilly or myself if she can't get you."

"And I know Abe and his men will head this way, if we ask."   Reilly paced, his eyes finally spotting the watch on the floor. He bent to pick it up.   "This isn't Redmond's."

Riordan studied it.   "And the techs searched this place.   How did they miss that?"

Reilly shrugged.   "I don't think that detective is trying too hard.   The team wasn't in here long enough to search much or take much evidence."

Riordan frowned. "You're right." He sighed.   "Find our team and send them in. They're not trained in crime scene details but they're thorough."

"I know. I put in a call to them." Rory walked away, his thoughts dark.

"Okay, sons. Once they're here, we'll head for the office. It's now become home base."

The families worried and worked, trying to find any information they could. Emma threw them what she had, Abe had been around, and his men had walked through the towns, listening and searching, all for naught. There was no sign of the three, and the families realized that Redmond and Shamus must have fallen victim to Sloane's kidnappers.

Shanley looked up from a chart he was working on as a nurse rushed towards him two weeks later.

"Debbie?"

"Shanley!   I just got word. They found Shamus. They're heading this way with him."

Shanley was on his feet, and then paused. "Find Victor. He's around here somewhere. I can't treat Shamus, but Victor will."

Victor finally stepped away from Shamus, finding Shanley waiting. Shanley's shift had ended but he refused to leave.

"Shanley? I need to grab a coffee. Come with me."

Victor sat, his eyes on his coffee cup before he looked at Shanley.

"Victor?" Shanley was almost afraid to ask, his eyes had assessed his brother from afar.

"He's in relatively good shape, Shanley. Bruising, which you would expect. His wrists are rubbed, I would say from handcuffs. He tried hard to get out of them. Dehydration. Malnutrition. We'll hook him up to some monitors and IVs and get him to a floor."

Shanley's eyes slid shut. Thank you, Lord, he thought. Shamus is home, and in one piece. Now to find the other two.

Chapter 35

William stood by his son's bed late that afternoon, seeing in the young man the boy who had dogged his footsteps, a question on his lips at all times. He gave a brief smile at how a simple answer was never enough for Shamus. His eye-lids slid closed as tears flooded his eyes for a moment. He stood, his arm around Anna, knowing Shanley was beside him, unable to even utter a prayer, he was so troubled.

His eyes opened once more as he watched Shamus move restlessly. The attending physician had told them Shamus had had to be sedated, he had kept trying to rise, to find Sloane. That worried William.

Riordan stood back, his eyes on his friend before dropping to Shamus. Thank you, Lord, that he is home and in one piece. Heal him. But please, dear Lord, let us find the other two before it's too late. We need to bring Sloane and Redmond home and soon. And direct our investigation, please, dear Lord? We're at a standstill. He finally turned and walked out of the room, not seeing Shanley's eyes on him before he followed.

"Riordan?" Shanley's voice stopped the older man who turned to watch him approach. "Have you talked to the police?"

Riordan snorted. "I did. They were not of much help. There was no evidence where Shamus was found. Dumped at the side of the road like so much garbage."

"That's what is bothering me. Why there?"

"At the side of the road leading to your parents's place? That was so strange. A warning, I think."

"You're likely right. Now, how do we find the others?"

Riordan shrugged. "We need to talk to Shamus. How long before we can?"

"I would say the morning. I'm planning on staying all night. Mom and Dad are heading back to the house late." Shanley turned to watch his brother's room. "Reilly said something about hanging around."

"He will. Aideen is with Naomi and Leah. Rory's desperately running names. Ryanne and Regan are on their way in." He sighed. "This is disrupting everyone's life. I wonder if that was the plan all along."

Shanley had turned to watch Riordan's face, his hand freezing on his neck where he had been rubbing it. "You could be right. Cause a lot of confusion and they get away. Now that we know their plan, what do we do?"

"We make some plans." Riordan shot a look back at the door. "I'm heading into the office.   Emma was to send in more material. Pray we find them soon, Shanley."

Shanley watched Riordan walk away before he too walked from the area, searching for the chapel. He slid into a seat at the back, his forearms resting on the pew back in front of him, his eyes on the lighted cross, before his head dropped to his arms. He heard slight movement beside him but didn't look up.

He was surprised as he heard an audible prayer, one that gave him hope and peace and strength to go on. He looked up, not seeing anyone there, but he knew someone had been. Just who, he wasn't sure. He stood, ready to fight on, before he paused, bending to pick up the paper that lay on the seat where he had been seated. He opened it, read it, and then was on the move, heading for his father and then to Riordan. Someone had just given them information that must might find the couple.

William looked over the paper, shaking his head at Shanley.

"I don't know that name, Shanley. I've never heard it mentioned here in town. Have you talked to Riordan?"

"I'm heading that way now, Dad. I'll be back in a couple of hours. I plan on staying all night. Reilly's in the waiting room. Call him if you need anything."

Anna watched Shanley walk away, before she turned back to Shamus. "William? What did we do wrong?"

"What do you mean, Anna?"

"I mean, Shanley's off on a mission, not related to his own profession. Shamus is laying here in a hospital bed, and we can't talk to him. Our only daughter is missing.

Where did we go wrong? And where is God?"

"Oh, Anna, love, He's here. He has promised to never leave us." William wrapped his wife in his arms. "Shanley has always had a drive for answers. That's why he went into medicine. Shamus? Now, Shamus, he's one we could never stop from hunting for answers or helping people. And I firmly believe Sloane is still alive. God has her in the hollow of His hand, both she and Redmond."

"I know that in my heart, William. It's my head that's having trouble."

"We overthink things, love. Here, have a seat. Let's pray. I know the churches are praying for us."

Shanley found his parents a few hours later, sending them off for the night with a promise to call when Shamus awoke. He settled down into a chair, knowing it would be a long night, not realizing how tired he was. He slept. He didn't see the figure that entered the room, stood over Shamus, and then rested a hand on his head before the figure moved out of the room. Reilly, heading that way, paused for a moment, a frown on his face. Did he know that man, he wondered? He shrugged, knowing the name would come to him at some point if he did.

He spread his papers out on the table he swung away from the bed, deep in his study, when he heard a sound and looked up, to find Shamus sitting up, staring around the room. He was on his feet, heading for him, when Shamus looked his way.

"Reilly? What on earth? Where am I?"

"You're in the hospital in town. We've set up shop, as you can see, in your room. Your brother couldn't stay awake."

Shamus looked over at Shanley. "No, he's been pulling a lot of shifts in Emergency, I think just to keep busy. And you?"

"I'm okay. But how are you?" His voice was kept low.

"I'm angry, Reilly. That's what I am. Where did they find me?"

"On the side of the road leading to your parents'."

Shamus nodded. "That's what I figured they'd do. I need out of here." He pulled at the IV, clamping a hand over the spot it had been in his wrist to stem the blood flow. "Where are my clothes?"

"Here. And here's a bandaid. I brought one, figuring you'd do what I would do."

Shamus gave a quick grin. "We think alike, I see. Rouse Shanley. We're leaving. I have someone I need to talk to."

The three men quietly walked away from the hospital, no one taking a second glance seeing Shanley leaving, thinking he was just finishing up a shift. Reilly sent a quick text to his father and then slid behind the wheel of his car, Shamus in the front seat, Shanley behind him.

"Where are we off to, Shamus?"

"Here. This address. I want to talk to that detective. His sister showed up at the first place we found."

"His sister? Then it's no wonder it seems like a shoddy investigation."

"What do you mean, Reilly?" Shamus shifted in his seat to watch him.

"I mean, we found a watch in Redmond's office that the techs should have found. I talked to one of them. They were told not to bother searching the office. In fact, the door was closed when they were there."

"He's hiding something. All right. Let's find him."

Chapter 36

The three men stood away from all the activity around the detective's house, a frown on each of their faces. What had happened, Reilly had asked? He finally slipped away, seeing an officer he knew.

His face was grim when he returned, pointing to his car, waiting until he was away from the area.

"Reilly? Care to share what you found out?" Shanley's voice finally broke the silence in the car.

"The detective's dead. The officer said it looked like a home invasion gone wrong, but they doubted that. They had headed to his place when word came in that he was the target of someone and they wanted to warn him. They hadn't been able to reach him on his phone, which was unusual." Reilly pulled to the side of the road, sending a quick text message to his family.

239

"And now, where does that leave us?" Shamus stared from the side window.

"Starting over, I would say." Reilly pulled away from the curb, heading where he had no idea.

"Reilly, head for our town. There's a place I want to check out." Shamus spit out the address. "I had been watching it for another reason, but something tells me it's connected to this."

"It is? Then, certainly, let's head there. First, though, we need food and coffee." He pulled into a local coffee shop that had a drive-through and placed their order, handing off the food and coffee as it came to him.

Reilly reached for his phone as it chimed, giving it a quick glance, before tossing it to Shamus. "Answer that and put it on speaker?"

Shamus complied, hearing Riordan speaking almost before he had answered.

"Reilly? Where are you?"

"Heading for Sloane's town. Shamus has an address we're checking out."

"Be very careful. They are trying to blame you for the detective's death."

"What?" Reilly pulled swiftly to the side of the road and slammed the ignition into park. "How?"

"Someone has reported a man fitting your description there about ninety minutes ago."

Reilly sighed. "That's how they're playing it. They'll find out I talked to an officer there twenty minutes ago. But at that time? I was in the hospital room, talking with one of the nurses and a security guard was at the door. I never left until we all walked out."

"I know that. The officer in charge is heading for the hospital to pull security tapes. He's afraid someone will tamper with it. Your car?"

"I have the ticket when I signed out. Here, Shamus, put it somewhere safe. If you have it, I can't destroy it, now can I?"

"You three need to be very careful wherever you go and whatever you do. Do not go in on your own. If you find them, call in the authorities."

"We will, Dad." Reilly was silent, his mind mulling over what he had been said. "When does Abe and his team arrive?"

"They're already here, working with us. Emma and that man she has in her office, Jace? They're here too. We think we're narrowing down the area where they may be."

"Don't count on that, Dad. They seem to be always one step ahead of us, and I for one would like to know why. I won't call unless I need to. In fact, I'm turning off my phone."

"No, don't do that. Mute it but keep it on. I need to be able to reach you."

Reilly remained silent before he reached for the phone, his hand muting it and then tucking it back into his pocket. "Mute yours as well, guys. We don't need any sound alerting them."

The three men watched the building for a while before Shamus finally ran towards it, ducked low, the other two men following. He tried a door, opening it and entering, his footsteps ringing back hollow in the empty rooms. They walked through, finding evidence of a hurried departure before they stood in the basement, seeing the evidence that the couple had been there. Shamus stood for a moment, his eyes on the scarf he knew had been his sister's, that lay near her bonds, blood spattered on it.

"They've hurt her, Shanley. How bad?"

Shanley nodded. "We need to get out of here and call it in. We can't stay in here, you do know that, Shamus? And no, leave the scarf."

They watched the emergency vehicles approach, the lights flickering through the dawning sky, before a detective approached them.

"Shamus? I didn't know it was you." Red Matthews reached to shake Shamus' hand and then Shanley's, his eyes on Reilly. "And who is this?"

"Reilly Stuart. His brother, Redmond, is married to Sloane and that's who's missing."

"I knew Sloane had married but I didn't know she was missing. How long?"

"At least two weeks. She was taken from her home. That was a botched investigation."

Red paused, his pen hovering over his notebook. "The detective that was killed? It was his?"

Reilly nodded. "It was, and he ran a pretty shoddy investigation. Our team found evidence they should have and didn't or weren't allowed to."

Chapter 37

Reilly turned as his father approached, Abe with him, as the three men still stood, watching the activity going on.

"Reilly? Did you find them?" There was hope in Riordan's voice, hope that died as he saw the grim look on his son's face.

"They were here, Dad, but disappeared. The authorities think it was a very hurried departure."

"That it likely was." Riordan watched as Abe moved around, his eyes not on the building, but on the land around, searching for what, the older man wasn't quite sure.

Reilly finally approached Abe as he stood, leaning against a tree, his eyes on his friends.

"Abe?"

"Reilly, were you inside?"

"Just briefly. Enough to search to see if they were there."

"Talk to me. What did you see?"

"Not a lot. The house has no furniture, which is strange. We could see some garbage, mostly food containers, on the main floor. In the basement, we could see where they were tied to support posts. The posts were rubbed at, two of them. I suspect that's where Redmond and Shamus were tied. Shamus found Sloane's scarf. At least, he was sure it was hers. There were blood spatters on it, how old I couldn't tell you." He slumped against a nearby tree, his voice quiet as he continued to speak. "This is so much like that last extraction. We need to find them, Abe, and soon."

"We will, Reilly. Don't lose hope. I have Micah searching. Kat, remember Micah's wife? She's running her family tree program, pulling names of relatives that we didn't even know about."

"She is? That's good. But how does that find them?"

"She has worked with numerous police forces. They track back families and see where they are, who they are, and how close they are to the suspects. Then, they go in and interview. This is new technology and techniques, Reilly. We've used it."

Reilly shrugged, not sure on that, as Shamus stopped beside him.

"Abe?"

"Shamus Everett? It's been a while." Abe reached to shake Shamus' hand. "Your sister?"

"Sloane is. I just wish I knew where she was."

"We're working on that. Emma's running through a number of addresses. Do you know the owners of this place?"

"Unfortunately, I do. I never expected them to be involved, but there have always been rumours. The Aldersons are well known in town, and have covered up a lot, from my investigations."

"That's what we're hearing and finding. Are they in town?"

Shamus shook his head. "They always leave town about this time of year for a few weeks. But what I don't get is why the house is empty. This is their principal residence."

"It is? And it's empty? That's something we need to work on. Would they have hired a moving company?"

Shamus snorted in derision. "They wouldn't lift their own fingers or dirty their own hands to move their belongings. They may have had a rental truck and had their men do it."

Abe nodded, his fingers busy on his phone as he sent the information on to Emma. "Emma will have someone look into that. Now, we need to get all of you out of here. Have they talked to you yet?"

Reilly nodded. "They did. They told us we could leave at any time but we were waiting for any information. It doesn't look as if it's forthcoming."

Riordan was reluctant to leave, the house the last connection to his daughter. He wanted to stay, to walk through the house, to see what he could find, but he knew he would not be allowed to. He let Reilly lead him away, tucking him into Abe's car, before heading for his own.

"Reilly? Where now?" Shamus' quiet voice finally broke the silence in the car.

"Where to? I have no idea." He shifted on his seat, a headache starting behind his eyes. "Somehow, I don't think they're in town. We need to figure out where they would be." He turned to Shamus, catching a look on Shanley's face. "Shanley? You have an idea?"

Shanley stared at him, before he nodded. "I do. I have heard rumours around the hospital of a cabin they have. I'm not sure where, though. I need to talk to Mike, the lead security officer."

"Where do we find him?"

Shanley squinted at his watch. "He'll be at home. He's always off on Tuesdays. And now I have to wonder why. Everyone else rotates, but he never does. He has the same days off every week."

Shamus jerked around to stare at his brother. "Tuesdays? That's when the enforcer would make his pickups of protection money. Is it Mike?"

Shanley shrugged. "It could be. We need to talk to him. Here's his address."

They stood back from the road, watching the activity around Mike's house.

"This doesn't look good." Shanley pulled out his phone as he felt it vibrate and paled as he read the message. "We won't get to talk to him."

"He's dead?" Shamus didn't wait for his brother to confirm his question. "They're removing people who can lead to them. What are they planning for Sloane and Redmond?"

Chapter 38

The families gathered in the conference room at Riordan's building, not sure where they were heading, but knowing time was running out for the couple. How did they find them?

Abe and his men stood and watched before Micah, Ian and Murphy approached Abe. A few minutes of quiet conversation and they left. Ian had an idea and he wanted the other two with him.

Emma stood for a moment, watching the families, before she approached Regan, pulling her to one side.

"Regan?"

"Emma? Where are they? We need to find them and find them fast. How do we do that?"

"I know. Ian has an idea he's running with."

"And that would be?"

"He's our pilot. He's off to rent a plane and scour the area from the air. He's hoping to find a cabin or shack or something we can search."

"He's done that?"

"He has. It's who they are, Regan. They do this for friends. Now, you. What can I do for you?"

"Just find my brother." Regan turned back to watch her parents, seeing the strain in them, the worry, and yes, she could see them giving up hope. "They're losing hope, Emma. How do we keep that up for them?"

Emma just shrugged, having no answers for her friend. "Ian will call or one of the others will if they find something. Listen, we need to find food for everyone. Do you have supplies or we can order in?"

"Order in." Regan led the way to her office. "I can call the deli in town. They'll send out an order."

Emma's hand stopped her. "No, let two of our guys go in and get it. Just hand them your order."

Regan stared at Emma for a moment before she nodded. "Of course. We need to do that." She quickly scrawled out an order and handed it to Emma. "Tell them that it's for Dad and they'll charge it to our account."

Riordan came looking for Regan, a question rising to his lips before he simply enveloped her into a hug, his eyes sliding shut. This was so much worse, he thought, than what the others went through. Even when Regan was missing for those weeks, they held out hope. Now, they didn't have that hope.

Emma walked away at that point, walked into Abe's hug, and heard his fervent prayer. God, we need You to show us where they are. We can't find them. I know they're alive but where?"

Abe pulled out his phone, holding it to his ear, his eyes on Emma before they slid closed. She feared the worse when he did that.

"Abe?" He hadn't spoken when he pocketed his phone. "What is it?"

"Ian spotted something. They're heading back to the airport and then are heading in to the area. He thinks it's a good four or five hour walk from here."

"And they won't use any machines." Emma looked around. "Do they want Shamus or Shanley?"

"He said no. Not right now. Not until they knew if it was them. And then he wanted our team to move in."

"Of course." Emma's heart dropped. "They think they're not alive?"

Abe nodded. "That's what I heard Micah muttering. Keep the faith, love. We need to do that." He nodded towards the group. "Here's the food. Let's eat and then I suggest we break into groups and pray."

"A solid idea." William stood beside Abe. Abe wondered afterwards how long he had been there but never dared ask and William never said.

Chapter 39

Ian paused, his eyes searching the area around the shack he had found from the air, his breath white in the cold. He rubbed his hands, knowing they were close to finding something. Just what, he wasn't sure?

Micah tapped his shoulder and pointed to the left side of the shack, Murphy to the right. They snuck away, finding no problem with cover. Ian moved towards the front door, his eyes on the path. It had been beaten down by numerous footsteps and he didn't think they were just ordinary citizens. Experience showed him there were female tracks in the mix, and that she was not steady on her feet. He waited, back to the wall, listening but not hearing anything. He reached for the door handle, finding it moving easily under his hands.

He shoved open the door, staying to one side, listening before he ducked in and dropped to the floor to one side, his eyes searching the building, seeing Murphy and Micah coming in the back.

It was empty, and his heart fell. They had prayed they would find them today, but it was not the case. The men rose to their feet, searching, finding stumbling almost by chance onto a journal. Micah looked through it.

"They were here, Ian. Murphy. They were here. We just missed them."

"How do you know?"

Micah held up the book. "It's in here. They were to hold them here until noon today and then move them. It doesn't say where, though. It can't be that far."

"No. It's only two now. We missed them by just that much." Murphy was frustrated and walked out the back door, his eyes on the horizon, before he paused, heading back into the shack. "Which way would they go?"

"Back towards town. They must have taken another trail. I don't remember seeing one." Micah was out the door, heading back down the trail, before running back to the other two. "Did they leave anything inside?"

"No." Ian walked towards him. "Did you find something?"

"I think so. There's another path. Off to the side. We didn't see it because you can't see it when you're walking in."

They shouldered their packs and walked quickly away, Micah finding the path and setting off at a quick pace. They finally paused, hearing voices ahead of them, and dropped their packs to the side of the path, before creeping forward.

They exchanged glances as they listened to the argument before they walked forward, surrounding the two men who stood, facing one another, voices raised in anger.

"Can we help you two?" Ian's voice cut through the conversation, drawing the men's attention to them.

"No, I don't think so. My friend and I are must having a conversation." The younger man tried to edge away but stopped as he saw Murphy standing close to him.

Micah had headed for the other side of the small clearing. "They went this way, fellows." He spun, a hard, stern look on his face. "And I think these two know where they've gone."

Belligerent, the younger man refused to talk. The man, who appeared a few years older, finally sighed and shook his head.

"It's over, Billy. They have us. We might as well talk."

"That would likely be a good idea. Where are they?" Ian's voice lashed out at him.

"The young couple? They took them out early this morning. I have no idea where they were heading, just that we were to wait and then follow along this path. They would be ahead of us somewhere."

"Did they tell you where to meet them?"

The man nodded, much to Billy's anger. "There's a clearing about five miles from here. We're to meet them there."

Billy made a sudden move to run back towards the shack, but was stopped by Micah's sudden tackle. Drawn to his feet, his hands were bound in front of him and he was shoved along the path. His companion walked quietly, knowing that they were captured and that cooperating just might work to their advantage.

Ian raised his hand finally, his eyes on the clearing. He motioned to Murphy, whose sudden movement of drawing a gag over Billy's mouth had the younger man fighting him before Murphy simply shoved him down and bound his feet.

"Keep quiet." Murphy's low growl had Billy suddenly realizing just how deep in trouble he was and he nodded, his eyes moving to his companion, who simply shook his head.

Ian and Murphy moved a few feet ahead, feet carefully placed, before they could see the men waiting. They searched, drawing a breath of relief as they saw Sloane and Redmond seated on separate logs, not bound. The two men exchanged glances before counting heads. Only three men guarding them, Ian noted. One for each of them, he thought.

They moved back quietly, their voices low as they conversed before they turned to their two captives, pulling them to their feet and to trees where they were tied, gags across their mouths, before the three men separated and walked around the clearing, seeking spots they could enter it without being noticed they prayed. Murphy noted the cliff to one side and prayed that no one headed that way. He didn't want to be the one having to climb down to retrieve a body.

Chapter 40

Redmond looked up at last, his vision blurry as he watched Sloane. He knew she was hurting in many ways, the hard tramp through the woods difficult for her. She had been beaten, that he knew. He had too but he just didn't understand why. They hadn't asked them for anything. In fact, he knew they hadn't asked for anything since that first day. He had awakened to find Shamus tied up near him and twisting around, he had found Sloane, who sat, head down on her knees, appearing to be asleep.

He had no idea why they had been moved to that shack two days ago or why now they were being marched back through the woods. Something had gone wrong with their captors' plans, he suspected, and he prayed that they would have a chance to escape. Only, they were watched too closely. He looked up further at that point, and a frown covered his face. He saw Ian as he approached the man in front of him, a quick movement taking him out and away.

Redmond was on his feet, reaching for Sloane when a sudden burning pain in his back, between his shoulder blades, sent him to his knees and then to ground, his vision blackening even as he heard Sloane scream.

Sloane watched in horror as the thrown knife embedded itself in Redmond's back. She was on her feet, backing away, not realizing how close she was coming to the edge. Micah moved towards her on a run, even as Murphy tackled the man heading for her and Ian took the third man down.

Sloane felt the earth giving away from below her foot as she took a last step backwards. She screamed, even as she tried to throw herself forward, her hands reaching for Micah's, desperate to grab on. To no avail! She tumbled backwards, a new scream wrenched from her, and then silence as the men heard her body land. Micah landed on this ground, his face burrowed into his arms, despair moving through him, before he crawled to the edge and looked over. He saw Sloane's body, ten feet, he thought, below him. He crawled backwards, his phone out, calling Abe, giving their location and asking for help.

Ian and Murphy were beside him, hands on his arms, preventing him from dropping over the edge.

"Micah! Wait. We have ropes and a harness in our packs. You know that. Let's get you fitted out before you go over." Murphy was already running for their packs, tugging out the equipment and then helping Micah into it. Ian searched for an anchor, finding a solid tree and tying off the rope before he was back beside his friend, work gloves pulled on and reaching once more to stop Micah.

"Wait. Prayer first."

Micah nodded. "How's Redmond?"

"It went deep, but I'm not sure how protected he was with his coat." Murphy looked back at Redmond. "Let's get you over and then I'll go assess him. Ian, how long before help?"

"Abe said maybe thirty. They'll fly them in by copter."

Micah carefully scaled down the wall, watching as bits of earth and debris broke away under his feet. He had stayed to the side, careful so nothing fell on Sloane. She had landed on a ledge but was unmoving. He feared that it was too late. He pulled a glove from his hand, and reached for her, hand shaking as he did so. His head dropped as he felt for a pulse.

He could heard Ian calling to him but he didn't look up for a moment, causing Ian to call in a more worried tone.

He finally looked up, breathing a prayer for the young woman.

"She's alive, Ian. I don't know how, but she is. Send down one of the blankets. I want to keep her warm until help comes." He reached for the rope that dropped the blanket, shoving it aside even as he braced himself against the cliff wall and carefully tucked the blanket around Sloane. His hand rested lightly on her back and he prayed that it would not be the thirty minutes Abe said, that help would be there sooner. He didn't think either one had a chance of making it if it took too long.

Ian backed away from the edge and dropped to a crouch beside Murphy.

"Murphy?"

"It's bad, Ian. I don't know if I can keep him alive to get him to help. He's bleeding heavily." Murphy had cut away as much of the jacket as he could and packed heavy bandaging around the knife. "I've done everything I can. I wish Matt was here."

"So do I, but he's not. And he would have to choose which one. Right now, we're looking after both. God will take care of them, keep them alive." Ian turned to look back towards the cliff. "Micah says Sloane landed on a ledge. He's trying to keep her as warm as he can until help comes." He reached for his phone, surprised that they had service. "It's Abe. Abe?"

"We're five minutes out. How are they?"

"Family?"

"No. We didn't tell them."

"Good. Then we can talk. Murphy's trying to keep Redmond alive. He was knifed in the back as he tried to get to Sloane. Sloane...." Here, Ian's voice dropped off.

"Ian? Sloane?" When Ian didn't answer right away, Abe's heart sank. "Ian? Is she alive?"

"She is. She went over the edge of a cliff. Micah's down there with her."

"Okay." Ian could hear relief in Abe's voice. "We're just about there. We have two teams of paramedics. Officers are coming in behind us in another copter and on foot."

"We have five suspects for them, Abe."

"Good. But not the leader."

"No. They were just sitting here, waiting. For what, I have no idea."

Murphy looked up, his head shaking. "Ian. We're near a cliff. Don't you think that was the plan?"

Ian's face paled, even as he tucked away his phone. "I get what you mean." He stood, a hard look in his eyes as he stared at the five men. The other two men had been brought to the clearing. "They are vindictive and cruel, aren't they?"

Chapter 41

Abe stood to one side, Ian beside him, watching as the paramedics worked to stabilize Redmond. Murphy refused to move from his side, standing watching, wiping at his hands to remove the blood. Abe wasn't sure how serious Redmond's condition was, but he could tell by the looks on his men's faces that it was bad. He finally moved towards Murphy, watching as IV lines and an oxygen mask was applied to Redmond before he was carefully lifted to a basket stretcher.

"I'm going with him, Abe." Murphy refused to look at him, his eyes on Redmond.

"I thought you would be. Go. I already cleared it for one of you to go with each one. I know Micah will want to go with Sloane. Ian?"

"I'm here, Abe. I need to talk to the officers before we head back in."

Abe nodded, his eyes watchful as Redmond was carried gently to the waiting copter, his stretcher fastened inside and then the paramedics and Murphy were closed in behind the doors and the copter lifted off and then headed for town. He walked back towards the cliff, his eyes watching Micah as he stood as near to the cliff's edge as he could get, his neck craned to watch the activity below him.

Micah had tilted his head back and watched the copters move in and land, the aircraft disappearing from his line of sight. He had heard the voices of the men and then saw the ropes heading his way. He refused to move until the two paramedics were beside him, their hands reaching for Sloane, assessing her. He had shaken his head when questioned if she had been conscious. He had slid to one side before finally pulling himself up to the surface but staying near enough that he could watch the men work. He turned as Abe touched his arm, drawing him back.

"Talk to me, Micah."

"She's alive, Abe. I don't know how, but she is. The paramedics don't hold out much hope, though." Micah kicked at a clump of dirt in frustration. "We have never lost anyone, Abe. Why now?"

"We haven't yet, Micah. I don't think we will. You know what Matt says. They expect the worst, prepare for it, but pray for the best. That's what we're doing. I want you with her when she goes in."

"As if you could keep me away." Micah turned back to watch, not hearing the men asking to be raised up yet. "Redmond?"

Abe shook his head. "He's away to the hospital. Murphy won't leave his side. I've sent Nathaniel and Matt to find the families. Emma's with them, even though she's still working away."

"I don't get it, Abe. Why move them like they did?" Ian was puzzled, trying to work out the why's of the move.

"I know. It doesn't make a lot of sense. Reilly said he feared something like this. He doesn't know yet that we've found them."

"He will soon enough. Make sure someone is with him. He's taking this personally." Micah walked back towards where the ropes were being pulled in, reaching out to help, his hands one of the first to reach for the stretcher, to help carry it to the waiting copter. He stared down at Sloane, whose head and neck were now stabilized to prevent movement, her body strapped to a back board. He prayed for healing for her. He knew it would take months for healing for her body, if she survived. He could tell from the grim looks that there was still a possibility that she wouldn't.

He did up his seatbelt, his eyes on Abe as Abe nodded before he turned to answer a question. Micah prayed as he watched the ground float by before his eyes once more sought Sloane. Her face had grown whiter, he thought, almost a gray look to it. He prayed for her family and for her husband.

He walked slowly into the Emergency Room, his head shaking as they tried to make him wait.

"No, I stay with her. I'm her security detail. If you have a problem with that, take it up with the police." He stopped in the room, stepping to one side, his eyes on the physicians and nurses as they worked. He knew Abe would find him when he could.

Emma looked up as Matt had approached her, hope in his eyes.

"Emma? Where are the families?"

She rose, heading away from the desk she had been using. "In the conference room. I think all of them are there. Why?" Matt didn't speak for a moment, and Emma feared the worst, that the couple had been found but were dead. "Oh, Matt! Don't tell me!"

"They're alive, Emma. Ian, Micah and Murphy found them. But they've been hurt. How bad, Abe didn't say, other than that they were on the way in with them. Ian and Abe are still out there."

Riordan looked up as the door opened and Emma peeked in, counting heads, before she pushed the door open all the way and entered, Matt on her heels. He was on his feet, approaching her, hope rising in his heart at the look on her face.

"Emma?"

"We have them, Riordan. We have them." Emma watched with compassion at the various reactions of the family members as they heard and then understood her words.

Riordan stopped, not quite sure he had heard her. He could hear the rustle and footsteps as the families approached, and felt Naomi's arms come around him. He started at Emma and then Matt, who nodded, a smile on his face.

"We have them, Riordan. Micah and Murphy are on their way in with them." Matt's hand was there to prevent Riordan's collapse to the floor as his knees buckled.

"You have them? They're alive?"

"They are. Abe didn't say much about their condition, but they are hurt. They're likely at the hospital now. We're making arrangements with your people to get you all there and keep you safe. You are all in danger now."

Riordan nodded, his arms tightening around his wife. "Okay, let's get us there. Matt, you are in charge right now. We're not up to watching for our safety, and that's dangerous." He looked around the room, tears briefly clouding his vision. "William?"

"Yes, Riordan, we do need to pray." William led them off in a prayer of thankfulness, praise, and petition, followed by the others in turn.

Matt watched as the families quickly filed into the Emergency Department, spreading out and finding seats, their eyes on the doors to the rooms. He turned as he heard footsteps. Abe stood beside him.

"Abe?"

"How are they? Other than the obvious?" Abe nodded towards the families.

"Hurting. They are worried. Riordan and William are trying to stay positive for their families, but they've been around the block too many times to know that things can still go wrong. How are they?"

"Redmond took a knife to the back. I heard from Murphy. They've taken him to surgery already." He paused, his emotions overcoming him for a moment. "Sloane went over a cliff. Micah tried to get to her but couldn't in time. Murphy and Ian had to restrain him from going over himself until he was in gear. She's hurt, Matt. We don't know how bad. Micah didn't seem to think she would make it."

Matt's eyes slid closed, knowing how much it took for Micah to admit that. "We'll pray, Abe. We'll pray like we never have before. Micah's still with her?"

"He is. I've been back. The faces are grim on the ones working on her. He'll come find me when they're ready for the family to go back." He looked up at that point from the keys he had been holding in his hands. "Micah?" Micah stood beside him, an unreadable look on his face.

"They want her family, Abe." Micah's voice held sorrow. "She's still alive, they don't know how, but they don't expect her to make it through the night." He blinked back tears. "Why? Do we even know why?"

Abe shook his head. "Not yet, but we're close. Emma sent word she had the final piece of what she needed to make sense of all this and name names. It's no consolation though, is it?"

Abe turned to walk towards William, finding the man on his feet, even as Micah headed back towards Sloane.

"Abe?"   Williams's voice held a mixture of hope, worry, and despair.

"The physicians have asked for Sloane's family to come back. They didn't limit how many, so if you'll come with me, I'll take you to her. Micah is still with her."

"Before we go, any word on Redmond?"   William looked towards Riordan, who stood near him.

"The last I heard, he was in surgery"

Chapter 42

Anna's hand rested on her daughter's, tears flowing down her cheeks, as she studied her face, before her other hand reached to touch the sunken cheek, the white skin, taking in the bruises, the nicks and cuts, the dark shadows under the eyes. William stood, his arm around his wife, his eyes on his daughter, anger beginning to burn in his heart. Shanley and Shamus stood on the other side of the bed, Shamus full of regret that he couldn't have gotten her away, Shanley, knowing what she faced, in despair.

The nurses finally moved them away, telling them that they needed to tend to Sloane. William turned away, his eyes searching for the physician, finding him standing watching them.

"Doctor? Be honest with me. How is she?"

The physician nodded towards an empty room. "In there, I think. We do need to talk. We'll be taking her to surgery. She has some broken bones to set and some internal bleeding we need to address."

William's arm was around Anna and he heard the two boys behind him. "Okay, now tell us. We want to know what she's facing."

The physician nodded. "Normally, I would be speaking with her husband, but can't. As I said, she has some broken bones. Her right femur for one. That in itself is life-threatening. She fractured that in her fall. Her wrist is broken, but that appears to have happened in the last few days, not today. We'll need to set that. Her back? I know there was concern about that. I don't see anything on the imaging studies that is concerning. That being said, she is bruised. She does have internal bleeding, we're not sure where from. It's not enough to be concerned that organs are involved, but we will go into the abdomen and assess that. She likely has a concussion, but I don't see any fractures of any of the bones. She is dehydrated, malnourished. How long has she been gone?"

"At least two weeks." Shanley spoke up at last, not saying what was on his heart, but knowing the battle his sister faced.

The physician nodded. "I'll have someone take you to the surgical floor." He turned to leave before he paused, looking back at them. "That young man with her?"

"Micah? He stays with her, even in the operating room. That's a given." William simply shook his head at the questioning look. "He's part of a friend's security team, and has assigned himself to watch her."

"That's what he said. It's okay. I just wasn't sure on the family's wishes."

"Like Dad said, it's a given, Doc. If he's not there, someone will be." Shamus stared the doctor down, watching as the man walked away. "Let's find the surgical floor. Likely, Riordan's are up there now."

The families waited, the hours dragging long and hard, the hands of the clock not seeming to move. Abe and his men moved among them, Emma finally reaching out to Abe and drawing him aside.

"Abe? I know who it is. They won't believe it though." Emma was worried, and Abe didn't think he had seen her like this before.

"Get your proof printed and then we'll talk. I have spoken with the police chiefs in both towns and they are waiting for your information. They have a good idea of who it is."

"That's the thing, Abe. We can't go to them. It involved men and women on both forces and not just in the lower ranks."

Abe rubbed at his face, even as he watched Rory and Reilly heading his way. "Then, we deal with what we have to deal with. Go, Emma. Bring me your proof." He kissed her and sent her on his way, standing upright as Rory and Reilly stopped in front of him.

"Do you know who did this?" Reilly's question wasn't a question, but a statement.

Abe finally nodded. "Emma does. She's gone to print off her proof and then we'll deal with it." He nodded towards the operating room doors. "Any word?"

"Redmond's in recovery. There wasn't as much damage as they feared. The knife missed the vital organs. It nicked an artery, though, but not removing it helped." Rory's voice held the fatigue he was fighting. "William's still waiting on word on Sloane."

Abe nodded before he looked around. "I'll be here, somewhere. Come find me when they're moved to a room." He walked away, not seeing the frustration on Reilly's face.

"Rory, did he just do that?"

"He did, Reilly. He needed to. We need to let him work his magic and solve this. I would suspect he's just waiting for Emma and then he'll talk to us. We'll have to wait for Redmond and Sloane to hear what they have to say. It will be hours, if not days, before that happens." Rory slumped back against the wall. "This is too much like when Dad and Regan were hurt."

"I know. I don't like this." Reilly watched as Shamus approached. "Shamus?"

"We've had word. They've taken Sloane to Recovery. They think a couple of hours and they'll have her in ICU." He nodded towards Abe. "What did he say?"

"That Emma has proof of who it is and that we need to talk to Sloane and Redmond."

Shamus just shook his head and walked away, heading for the stairs. He didn't see Nathaniel, one of Abe's men, follow him, until Nathaniel touched his shoulder and directed him to the cafeteria.

Chapter 43

All those weeks ago, Sloane had set her phone back down on the desk, a smile on her face, a softened look around her eyes. Redmond had called, simply to tell her that he loved her and to ask how her day was going. He certainly didn't like to be away from her, she thought. Her attention went back to the papers she had spread out on his desk, a quick glance at the clock letting her know she had a couple of hours yet to work. She didn't like to work too late, wanting to have their dinner on the go when he walked in just after five.

She was soon immersed in transferring data from the sheets to the program her father had someone write for them. It just made sense, she thought, and it was so much easier to do their reports. She was on the last few and would be done in thirty minutes, she thought.

She finally sat back. She had done it, she decided. All the old reports were now in the program and they could search as they needed to. She looked up as she heard a sound outside, a frown on her face, before she heard the front door slam open. She was on her feet, a scream in her throat, as the three men ran into the office. She backed away from them, fear coursing through her as they advanced on her. She struggled against the grip one took on her arm, trying desperately to escape, to avoid the syringe another held in his hand, unable to do either. She felt the needle plunge in her flesh and then the world darkened as her vision faded and her body relaxed, gathered into one of the men's arm as she was carried swiftly from the room. She didn't see the photo placed on the bookshelf, a reminder to Redmond that he was being watched and by whom.

She roused slightly early the next morning, struggling to free herself, hearing soft moans and not realizing they were coming from here. She didn't see Redmond and Shamus tied to the support posts before she dropped back into the well of unconsciousness.

She roused again hours later, this time her eyes staying open, as she looked around, her eyes finally landing on Shamus tied near her. She tried to move towards him, to wake him, but couldn't. She tugged at her bonds, finding the cuffs grating against her wrists. Her head turned, and she stilled, seeing Redmond near her as well, his head back against the post, his eyes closed.

Lord, she prayed, let us out of here. Please, dear Lord? At least let the two men get away. She didn't look up as feet appeared in her line of sight and her eyes closed as her hair was roughly grasped and her head pulled backwards. She didn't understand the words shouted at her in a coarse manner. She slipped away once more into the darkness, not feeling her head roughly slammed against the post.

The men stood over the three of them, not happy that they could not interrogate any of them. They each knew that the leader of their group wanted answers, wanted papers of some kind that only the woman could provide, and now they could not even ask her for them.

The three were pulled from the basement of the house day after day, one at a time, and questioned, Sloane taking the brunt of the questioning. She was puzzled.

She kept re-iterating that she had not papers, no jewels, nothing that she was asked for. She never had. She watched closely one day, seeing shadowy movement in the dirty window, reflecting from behind her. The form seemed familiar but another question drove the impression from her mind.

There came a day when Shamus was pulled to his feet and taken upstairs. She waited for him to return, sharing looks with Redmond. They were not allowed to talk to one another, blows and deprivation of food and water their punishment if they did. She watched but Shamus had disappeared. Sorrow grew in her heart. She was sure he was dead. That sorrow changed to worry about Redmond and that worry led to despair. She tried to pray, to ask for protection, for release but God seemed deaf to her pleas.

Redmond watched Sloane carefully, his arms pulling at his wrists as he tried to slip his cuffs but he couldn't. He had an idea of what the men wanted, but knew that they would never get the paperwork. The jewels, though. He frowned at that. How did they know about them? His family had searched and had found no evidence of a theft of uncut stones, leading them to believe that whoever hid them had been the true owners and they would likely never track that person down, it had been too long.

He had prayed too for release but knew it was unlikely that it would come soon. He had seen this too many times. He feared for Shamus when the other man disappeared, his eyes on Sloane as she watched hourly for her brother to come back, finally drooping back against the support, knowing he wouldn't be there. He too saw shadowy forms when he was questioned, but could not place them.

Then the day came they were dragged from the basement once more and this time shoved into a van. He felt the movement of the van through traffic before it picked up speed on a highway. It finally pulled off the road and he heard the crunch of gravel under the tires. The doors slid open and they were forced from the vehicle. He blinked in the sunlight, staring around, his heart sinking as he realized they were out in the bush, near a trail. He saw her recognition of the area. She looked over at him, shaking her head slightly. She knew that this was likely it for them, he thought.

They were forced to walk, single file, separated by one of their captors, to a decrepit shack and forced down on chairs, their hands bound to the chair. No words were spoken by the men, not in the shack. He could hear their low conversation outside.

Two days later they were once more on the move, heading back towards the edge of the forest but on a different trail. He could see the agitation in Sloane, and wondered what it was she knew. They were finally forced to sit on two logs, across a clearing from one another and then the wait seemed to begin. The men paced. Redmond frowned. There had been five with them, but now there were only three. The other two seemed to have been left at the cabin.

He heard the men' conversation and accusations but kept his focus on Sloane. He knew she was hurting, not just physically, but couldn't reach her to help her. He looked past her and froze. Ian? What was he doing there? He watched as Ian silently took out one of the men and then he sprang towards Sloane, intent on taking her to the ground and not letting harm come to her. He heard her scream even as intense pain hit him in the back, driving him to the ground and into darkness.

Sloane had despaired of getting away. She saw how close they were to the cliff and her heart sank, knowing what the plan was for them. Over the cliff and no one would know. At some point in the future, their bones would be found and they would identify them, maybe but no one would know for sure what had happened. She saw Redmond on his feet, flinging himself towards her, before he was on the ground. She screamed, on her feet, backing away from the man advancing towards her, not realizing how close she was to the cliff. She heard someone call her name and saw Micah, she thought it was, throwing himself towards her, his hands outstretched for her to grasp. She felt the earth crumble under her foot and screamed again, trying to throw herself at Micah, but too off balance to do that. Her scream ended abruptly as she hit the ledge and lay still, pain wracking her body before she too slipped away into darkness,

Redmond's head turned restlessly on the pillow, and he tried to turn to his back, prevented from doing that by the bolsters at his back. His eyes blinked open and he tried to focus. He could heard someone calling him by name but he slipped away into darkness once more, leaving his sister, Regan, bent over his bed, her hand on his face, trying to force him awake again.

She looked around at Delaney, who stood, his eyes on her, not her brother.

"It's okay, Regan. He'll wake again. Come on. Our time's up in here." Delaney's arm around her drew her from the room, where she found her parents waiting.

"He was awake, Mom. Dad." Tears flowed as she sought her mother's arms, her father's arms around them. "He didn't stay awake, but his eyes opened."

Delaney looked past the three of them at the rest of the family gathered there, seeing the relief on their faces, knowing that

Redmond had roused. They had no idea yet what he faced or what the two had been through but at least he was rousing.

William stood watching as well, his heart glad for the Stuarts, but hurting for his family. There had been no movement from Sloane as yet, and although they were told that was expected, he still wanted her awake and talking. He wanted the people responsible. Then he heard the soft voice saying that vengeance was the Lord's, and he sighed again. It was.

He frowned as he stared at the man hovering near the entrance to the ICU waiting room and walked towards him.

"Walter Evans?"

"William. It's been too long. We need to talk."

"We do, Walter. Your family seems to have been wrapped up in what's happened."

"I know. I didn't know. I've lost my son to this. And my daughter refuses to talk to me. She's deep into this somehow too."

William drew the older man aside, seeing Abe nearby. "Here, let's sit and talk. This is a friend of mine, Abe. He needs to hear what you have to say as well. Wait. I'll be right back." William found Riordan and motioned him to follow him. "Riordan, this is Walter Evans."

Riordan nodded, making the connection. "What can you tell us?"

Walter talked and the men let him. He gave them information they needed, must to his distress. He had no idea his family had been deep into crime. It wasn't how they were raised. He finally rose, wiping at the tears on his face with a ragged bandanna, walking away a broken man. William watched him go, knowing that but for God, that could have been him with his family.

Riordan rose and paced, finally turning to Abe. "Is this enough, Abe? Can we make a case?"

"We might be able to. I need to talk the authorities again. I have all that information that Emma's been finding as well."

"Talk to them. Do it tonight, please? They've set up a room just outside here where they've been working." William walked away, leaving Abe staring after him, before he turned to Riordan.

Riordan pointed to the doors. "Let's go find whoever it is we need to. We can't let this rest. Not anymore. It's taken too much from our families. We'll heal but we'll never be the same." He looked back down the hall, towards his family and Sloane's. "It's taken too much from them."

Abe shook his head. "They'll be changed, that's a given, but they will come through. I've had too many friends go through this. You don't know Emma's and my story. We married quietly just before we graduated college. Long story short, her step uncle wanted her money. He told her I was dead, told me she wanted nothing to do with me. It took ten years for us to reconnect. We came through stronger and more in love than if we hadn't been separated. All of my friends would say the same."

"You did? You would never know it." Riordan paused. "And all your men?"

"Them and some friends of ours as well. I know some who would be willing to talk to both Redmond and Sloane when they want."

"Thank you, Abe. We'll keep that in mind. Now, let's see what we can do about solving this."

Chapter 45

Her eyes opening slowly, Sloane moved, groaning as she did so, her hand reaching for her leg and finding the cast. She sighed. What did she go and do that she could not remember going and doing? And just where was she anyway?

Her hand moved and she stared at the rings on it. What did these mean? She wasn't married. She didn't date, never had. She tried to sit up, a wild look on her face, before hands reached to hold her down. Her mother's face swam into her line of vision.

"Mom? Where am I?"

"In the hospital, honey. You were hurt."

"I know but these?" She held up her hand and then let it sink back, her eyes closing as she slept.

Shamus stood beside his mother, a frown on his face. "What did she mean? The rings?"

"I would suspect she's not remembering Redmond."

"That's not good. He's been asking for her, Rory said. They're having quite a time keeping him quiet and in the position where he can't hurt the incision. It's been what, two days?"

"Two days out of a lifetime." Anna's hand rested on his arm. "You need to work, Shamus.   Didn't you say you had investigations you needed to get to?"

"I do, Mom, but I don't want to leave."

"Sloane would tell you to do just that. Please? At least, head for your office and see where you stand with your work."

Shamus finally agreed, albeit reluctantly, and walked away, not seeing Shanley heading his way.

"Shamus?"

"Shanley.   Where did you come from?" Shamus stared at his brother, realizing he hadn't kept his mind on his whereabouts.

"Right here. Where are you heading?"

"Mom's kicked me out. She told me to head for my office."

Shanley nodded. "You need to. You've been away from it too long. I know you have an colleague who's been helping but you need to take back control."

"Sloane was awake, Shanley. She asked Mom about her rings."

"That's natural. Given what she's been through, she'll realize things in stages. Don't be surprised at the questions she'll ask."

"But she'll remember, won't she?"

Shanley shrugged. "I suspect she will."

Riordan watched the two young men walk by him before he glanced at Redmond's door. The nurses were changing dressings or something, he was told, and he would have to wait. Redmond was getting restless, wanting up, wanting to find Sloane. He didn't blame him. He would be the same, given similar circumstances. He had sent his family home, telling the two girls and Rory to go home, he would call if he needed them to come back. He headed for

Sloane's room, a hand pausing on the door as he prayed, before he quietly entered, startling Anna as he did so.

"Riordan? Redmond? Is he worse?"

Riordan just grinned. "No, they're doing something or other to him. How's Sloane?"

"She was awake briefly a bit ago. That's encouraging, I think."

"It is. And we can take whatever it is she says. I've been there with all of mine. As long as she doesn't say she was run over by a dinosaur, we're good."

"A dinosaur? Did you really just say run over by a dinosaur?" Anna stared at him as he broke out into laughter.

"A dinosaur. Ryanne insisted when she awoke the first time in the hospital that she was run over by a dinosaur. And she laid claim to Shea that day, without realizing that's what she had done. Redmond and Shea tease her about that all the time."

"She didn't! She doesn't seem the type to lay claim to anyone, not like that."

Riordan laughed even harder. "You have to understand that with Ryanne, being the youngest, she claims her stuff as she calls it and won't give it up. Apparently she called Shea "him" and that she needed him to keep her safe."

Anna shook her head even as she smiled. "They make a cute couple. You can see with your family how God has blessed each one with the life mate he had in mind for them." She looked back at Sloane. "That's how it is with Sloane and Redmond. I don't think we would have chosen the other for them, but God knew who they needed."

"He did at that, Anna. Listen, I have to run. I'm heading back to the office for a bit. Naomi's in the waiting room, I saw as I came in."

"That's good. I need to leave here for a bit. We'll just keep each other company."

Chapter 46

His hand on Sloane's, Redmond pulled himself to his feet, bending over her to brush back her hair, his hand resting on her face. His love for her had grown, and now that he could finally see her, he was glad. She moved restlessly at his touch, and he sat back down, fatigue weighing him down. They had both been moved to regular rooms, after a week, and he was content to spend as much of his day with her as he could. The nurses made him rest, but he fought them on that. Shanley had finally laid it on the line for him. He needed his rest, to be able to recover. Sloane needed that from him.

Redmond's head bowed as he prayed, his prayer a mixture of his own words, verses he knew, and silence. He finally dozed off, his head back on the chair, not seeing Sloane moving as she awakened.

Sloane stared around the room, not sure yet where she was, and sighed. A hospital room. At least it was that, she thought, fragments of memories haunting her. The basements of the building, the shack, and the clearing. She caught glimpses of men and felt herself falling. She jerked wider awake, her movements sending pain through her leg. Her head turned and she froze.

She watched Redmond as he slept, a frown on her face, as fragments of memories about him tickled at her mind. Then she glanced down at her hand and the rings and remembered. Redmond Stuart. Her husband. But what had happened to them? Something bad had, she knew. She remembered more and more, fear driving the memories to her mind quicker and quicker. She drew in a deep breath and blew it out. God, are You there? Did You protect us after all? You kept us alive, but is it over yet?

Redmond stirred once more, not sure what had awakened him, but keeping his eyes closed, he listened to the conversation going on around him. That was Regan, he thought. No, not Regan. He didn't know the voice but he could hear Sloane's responding and joy went through him. His sweetheart was awake.

He cracked his eyes open, not recognizing the young woman standing there. Sloane seemed entranced with the conversation before she looked over at him, a smile lighting her face.

"Redmond, love, you're awake. You need to meet Micah's wife, Kataleen. I'm sorry, Kat. She's been trying to help solve our mystery."

Redmond stood, reaching to shake Kat's hand, his head tilted. "Micah's wife? The one with the family tree stuff?"

Kat laughed at that. "That would be me. I can't stay, Micah's waiting for me, and we're heading away for a few days. But I wanted to stop by and leave material for you. And Sloane, if you need to talk, here's my card. Call me."

She walked away, leaving Redmond and Sloane staring at one another, not sure at that point what to say to each other.

"Redmond, you scared me when you went down. I thought you were dead." Sloane reached to hug her husband. "Thank God you're alive."

"Yeah, well, I don't know as I'd do that again. It hurt. Regan tells me the knife could have killed me. But what about you? I'm glad, I think, that I didn't see you go over the cliff. Ian said they had to keep Micah from going over after you until he had his harness on."

"He did that? I didn't know." She hugged him tighter. "Did they solve our mystery yet?"

"I think they're near to that. Dad said they were waiting for you to wake up so they could talk to you."

"Well, I'm awake. At least, I think I am. I feel like we've been living in a dream."

"Maybe, but from now on, we're not living in a dream."

"We're not?" Sloane frowned at him.

"We're not. We're going to be living our dream. Life is too short, sweetheart. I almost lost you."

"And I you." She looked around him as the door opened. "And here is Shamus. Shamus?"

Shamus' face lit up as he realized his sister was awake and he stepped up to hug her, holding her a little longer than he normally would.

"Welcome back, hon. Now maybe we can solve this."

"Not right now. Both of you two men need to leave. Redmond, your nurse is looking for you. Shamus, your father's on his way down the hall. He was looking for you." Sloane's nurse bit back a laugh at the looks on the men's faces. "You can come back. We just need a bit of time with Sloane. That's all." She winked at Sloane, causing Sloane to choke back her own laughter.

Chapter 47

A week later, Sloane settled herself on the couch in Redmond's home office, not willing to be too far from him. He had work he needed to do, that he just couldn't put off any longer. He looked up as she set her book aside and closed her eyes, a prayer of thankfulness on his lips. They were home, although the leaders of the gang that had attacked them and kidnapped them were still out there. He had refused Abe's offer to have his men stay or have the couple move to his security compound until the people were caught. Redmond knew that would never happen if they stayed hidden.

Dusk was creeping in as he finally stood, stretching, finding the movement not as hurtful as it had been. He stopped by the couch, his eyes on Sloane before he stooped and kissed her, leaving her sleeping. He stood for a moment in the kitchen, before he reached to make fresh coffee and then the hot chocolate Sloane preferred, setting their mugs on a tray with a plate of sandwiches and some fresh fruit. He headed back for the office, not seeing Sloane at first, but hearing her heading back his way, muttering as she worked her crutches. He knew she would be glad to be rid of them.

He helped her to a sitting position on the couch, propped up her leg, and then sat close to her, his arm around her as he prayed. She stared at the food, taking the mug he handed her, but starting to shake her head at a sandwich before she sighed and took one, nibbling at it.

"Do we need to talk again, Redmond?"

"About what?"

"About what happened? Dad says whoever it was has disappeared."

"Not for long. I talked to the investigator earlier. He says they have the warrants they need and addresses to serve them at." He bit into his sandwich, chewing before he swallowed, his eyes on Sloane. "Sloane, we have never talked about what we went through."

"No, we haven't." She sighed. "And we should. I just don't know why it happened."

"I don't either. It's not like they wanted anything from us, not that I could see."

She shook her head, sighing as the doorbell rang. "We weren't expecting anyone, were we?"

"Our mothers. They both said they'd stop by." Redmond headed for the door, pulling it open and then freezing, his hands rising as he saw the weapon pointed towards him, backing up as the men approached.

Forced to the floor of the kitchen and then bound hand and foot, he heard Sloane's protests at his treatment and then silence. He waited for the men to return but they didn't. He couldn't hear Sloane and that scared him. Not again, Lord, please not again.

Anna and Naomi exchanged glances as the door swung open in front of them before then entered, searching the house, Naomi dropping to her knees beside Redmond, undoing his bonds. He sat up, rubbing at his wrists, fear rising once more as Anna came back, a puzzled look on her face.

"Redmond, where's Sloane?"

He was on his feet, and out the front door, searching, finding one of her shoes, standing staring at it as his father approached.

"Redmond?"

"She's gone again, Dad. They took her again."

Riordan sighed, knowing that the warning he had just received and sent him this way had come too late. "They told me they were heading this way."

"Who did?"

"Whoever it is that's after her. How long?"

"Ten minutes, max. Mom and Anna just missed them."

"Okay, then we'll work that. The investigator is heading for a building they think is the headquarters."

"That's why, Dad. They have a source somewhere that's feeding them information." He looked up as vehicles slid to a stop and doors popped open. "And here is Abe."

"Redmond?" Abe stopped quickly beside Redmond, his hand resting on the other man's shoulders.

"They took her again, Abe. Ten minutes or so."

Abe nodded. "Was she wearing the bracelet you gave her?"

"The emerald one?" At Abe's nod, he thought about that. "She was. Why?"

"Because Micah worked some magic. He was able to put a GPS on it. All she has to do is touch a certain stone and it will activate it." He spun as he heard his name and found Joseph running towards him. "Joseph?"

"We have a signal, Abe. We need to move now."

Abe and his men were off, leaving Redmond and his father staring after them, even as patrol vehicles approached.

"What did he just say, Dad?"

"He's able to track her. Pray, Redmond, that she hasn't lost the bracelet." He turned his son back towards the house. "Inside. We'll wait there."

Abe watched as Nathaniel scoped out the building through a long lens. Nathaniel would stand guard outside, his weapon at the ready. He was the sniper on Abe's team, even though his talents had never been used in that way.

"She's in there, Abe. Tied to a chair in the centre of the room. By herself. I don't like this. It's a setup."

"I think you're right. It is a setup." Abe turned as he heard an exclamation from Luke. "Luke?"

"There are hot spots, Abe. Not from people."

Abe paled. "Hot spots?"

"Hot spots. Like they've planted explosives with timers."

"Can we get to her?"

"We can, if we're careful. I can track you through them." Luke studied the building, and what he was seeing on his monitor. "It doesn't look as if the back of the building has been set up with explosives. I suggest we go in through the front and then head for the back." He looked up at Abe.

Abe nodded, a grim look on his face. "I'm going in. Walk me through it. Some of you head for the back and work that window loose. I'll head that way once I have her. Is she moving?"

"No. I can't tell if she's conscious and too scared to move or if she's unconscious."

Carefully following Luke's words in his earpiece, Abe moved slowly through the building until he reached Sloane, finding her eyes on him, sheer terror in them. He laid his finger to his mouth, motioning that he would cut her free and then pointing to the rear of the building. She nodded, knowing that he couldn't go back the way he had just come. He reached for his knife, studied the ropes binding her and with quick motions, cut her free, sweeping her into his arms and heading for the back wall, Luke's voice in his ear, once more directing his steps. He handed her through the window into Matt's arms, who ran from the area, heading for their vehicle. Abe's hands found the window frame and he felt himself pulled through, landing lightly on his feet and then running away. They seated themselves in the van, Ian at the wheel, and sped away, the sudden shock of an explosion behind them rocking the vehicle.   They exchanged glances before Abe turned to Sloane, finding an angry young lady staring back at him.

Chapter 48

Redmond simply swept Sloane into his arms, not asking what had happened when she returned home. That had been three days ago. She refused to talk about it, but he could feel the anger in her. His prayer was for her to release the anger, and let God work in her heart. Over the past day, he could see that happening.

He helped her from his car that day at the office building, walking beside her as she struggled with her crutches, his hand out at the ready to help her. He held the door for her and then led her to the elevator, his heart sinking at the rebellion he saw in her. Not now, Sloane. Please, Lord, let us end this. If we don't she'll not heal and she needs to do that.

His father looked up from where he was seated in the conference room, watching as Sloane made her way around the room, finally stopping at a paper. He nodded. That was the one she had pointed to weeks ago, one with names that they had been working through. He had heard from the investigator just before the couple appeared. They had arrested all the men and women involved, including the leaders. Sloane had been right, after all. With her certainty on that and unbudging in her determination to prove it, that had led him and Emma to investigate more closely. Emma's work had been passed on the two forces and their investigators had worked through it, finding Emma had been very thorough in her research. Riordan had expected nothing different.

He finally rose and approached Sloane, Redmond hovering nearby.

"Sloane? Can we sit?"

She stared at Riordan before she sighed. "Whenever someone says that, it's always bad news."

Riordan began to laugh, finding Sloane's humour returning. "It does, does it? Humour me. You need to rest that leg."

She stared down at the cast as she sat. "No, I don't. I need to use it and can't." She felt Redmond's arm come around her and she reached to grasp his hand. "You have news?"

"I do." Riordan watched her closely, then shifted his glance to Redmond, finding his son's eyes on his young wife. "I do have news. I spoke with the investigator just before you came in. It's over."

The two stared at him, dumbfounded at his words, not quite sure they had heard him correctly.

"It's over, Redmond, Sloane. They've made the final arrest. They have solved your mystery and in doing so, solved the mystery of that last trip, Redmond."

Sloane slumped back against Redmond, not sure if she had heard correctly. "It's over? They've arrested them?"

"They have, Sloane. There's still some work to do, but I am told the culprits won't be out for a bit. You're safe, for the first time in years. It goes back a lot farther than you thought, back further than that body you found."

"Do we know who, Dad? And do we know why?"

"We do, Redmond. We know the answers to both."

"Can you tell us or do we need to wait?" Sloane leaned forward, her hands clasped together.

"I have permission to tell you. But first, let me get your chocolate and our coffee." Riordan was on his feet and then back in short order, the rest of the family and Sloane's family with him. She didn't see Abe, Emma and his men slip in quietly behind them. Her focus was on Riordan.

"First, let's pray. We need healing and peace about this. It's very disturbing."

Riordan finally raised his head, his eyes on his oldest son, remembering Redmond as an inquisitive child. When did he grow up, Lord, and become a man? A man married, who has been through hell and back, not just once? And Sloane, such a wonderful helpmeet for him.

"Redmond, Sloane. The person who was behind it? Not the Aldersons. Not the Evans. It was Dick Wight."

"Dick?"   Redmond's surprise was echoed by his family. "I thought he was a friend of yours."

"An acquaintance, son. Never a real friend. There has always been something about him that stopped me from getting close to him. Now, I know why. He's evil, through and through. Your father knew him as well, Sloane. He had tried to take over your father's company, hoping to use it for his smuggling but your father refused. That set Wight up to seek revenge on your father.

"As for our company, he had tried to obtain a position with us, thinking that he could use our company to hide his activities. He set up that last extraction, Redmond, seeking revenge against us. He had the young lady killed before you got there, planning to have you there at the time, but you were delayed. God saw to that. You would have been arrested, you and Regan, and spent time in prison overseas. It would have been very difficult to prove you didn't commit the murder.

"As to the rest of his activities, we've tracked back his smuggling, his money laundering, his robberies. He was behind the protection racket in our towns, hoping to drag us into it but never could. The investigator, Evans? He was his muscle in the protection racket. Evans never really investigated anything, which is what we thought all along. Evans' sister was married to Wight's son. His son was killed overseas in a robbery gone bad. Evans' sister was trying to blackmail Wight. She's disappeared and they're now looking for her body.

"That day in the clearing? The men were just waiting for word from Wight. The plan was to send you both over the cliff, which is what you suspected, Sloane. Abe's men moved in too soon."

Riordan paused, watching the looks on their faces, his eyes raising to watch the others in the room, seeing the relief that it was over, disbelief on most of their faces at who he had named, and concern for the young couple in front of them. Abe caught his eye and nodded. Riordan sighed. That meant the last person had been found.

"Sloane, that friend of yours from high school?"

"Which one?"

"A young lady named Yvonne?"

"Yvonne? We weren't friends. Just shared classes." She paused in her speech, her eyes on Riordan. "She's the voice I heard, the woman in the shadows."

"She was."

"Was?" Sloane turned to Redmond, finding his arm tightening on her. "She's dead?"

"She is. She was in the wrong place at the wrong time in Toronto. We have evidence she was trying to fence jewels she had stolen from Wight. We can't prove it, but the investigators think he had her killed."

"Evil. Pure evil. And hatred. I've seen him around town. He spewed that without even saying a word. No one wanted to be around him." Sloane had shifted in her chair and saw the others in the room. "Dad? You used to talk about him."

"I did. I never liked him. Never trusted him." He looked past her at Riordan. "Anything further?"

Riordan shook his head. "That's the basics of what I was told. There will be further information forthcoming, I think. The investigator will be keeping in touch with you two, updating you as needed. You will need testify in court at some point, but we'll work through that." He rose as he finished, and walked from the room, his shoulders stooping, the weight of what had happened on them.

Sloane looked after him and then was on her feet, following him.

"Riordan? Dad?" She hadn't realized that she had changed her name for him.

Riordan's steps stopped, his face showing his surprise as he turned, finding Sloane behind him.

"Dad? It's not your fault. You didn't know this would happen. You didn't know the character of the man or what he was capable of."

Riordan shook his head. "No, none of us did, I guess." He reached to hug her. "Have I told you how glad I am you're in our family? As Redmond's wife, you are not our daughter in law. You are our daughter in love. You have such a heart for people, Sloane. We all see that." He stepped back, made sure she was steady on her feet and then turned, walking away.

Redmond wrapped Sloane in his arms, pulling her back against him, his chin on the top of her hair. "Dad has spoken, sweetheart."

"I know. He's near tears, Redmond. How do we help him?"

"Just let him by himself for a bit. Mom will find him. This is what can happen with him. He walks away to find a prayer corner for himself."

"He does? That's a good way to handle this." She turned in his arms. "It's really over?"

"It is. Now, come back with me to the conference room. We need to celebrate. We'll do it quietly of course but we have friends and family who want our company."

Two months later, Redmond searched the house, not finding Sloane. He paused, knowing that it wasn't the past revisiting them. He had heard today from the investigator. All the ones that had been arrested had pled guilty, including Wight. That meant they didn't have to appear in court or testify against them. It would have been closure for them, he knew, but they really didn't need it.

He paused, his head tilting as he heard soft mutterings and then a soft voice singing one of his favourite hymns, the one about finding a refuge in a storm. He tracked the voice, finding Sloane sitting on the back deck, enjoying the spring sunshine, her legs curled up under a blanket. He leaned against the wall, just watching her for a moment, before he headed her way, sweeping her into his arms and sitting back down in the swing, setting it in motion with his foot, content to just be there, holding his wife, knowing how close it had been to either one of them not being there.

"You're home early, love. Dad kick you out of the office?" Sloane's voice held the smile she was trying to hide.

"Nope. He told me to leave and find a certain wife and take her out on the town, at his expense."

"Fancy dress, is it?"

"That would be it. That soft yellow dress."

"And your tux, of course." She snuggled down against him. "God has been good, hasn't He?"

"He has, sweetheart. That hymn you were singing? About a refuge in a storm?" He felt her head nod against his chin. "That was just so true for us. We had to find that refuge. If we hadn't and God had not kept us, we would not be sitting here."

"I know. It still scares me at times, if I let it. He has taught me so much about depending on Him and Him alone."

They sat in silence for a while before Sloane shifted again. She still had discomfort in her leg at times and had been told she always would. She sighed to herself. So much for what she had planned for her life. God had other plans, it seemed. Riordan had asked if she would join their business, teaching search and rescue as it would relate to their business. She had asked for time to pray about it but knew she would agree. It would mean working with Redmond but that she could do.

"Sloane, I heard from the investigator today."

She shifted again, her face tilting up to him, finding he was staring ahead, not looking down at her, an unreadable look on his face.

"When do we have to testify?"

"We don't."

"We don't? But I thought we had to." Sloane was confused.

"No, they have all taken plea deals, including Wight. There was just too much evidence against them."

"I'm glad. I really didn't want to face them in court."

"Nor did I." Redmond waited before he spoke again. "Can we do something for our families?"

"Like what?" She felt him shrug, knowing he was uncertain as to what he wanted. "We can but there is something else I'd like to do."

"And that would be?"

"I want to walk down the aisle to you, on my feet. I know we're already married, but our family missed out on that."

"I know. So, why don't we plan a celebration for them. A lunch or something and we can combine your desires with that."

She looked up at him, finding his eyes on her before he kissed her thoroughly

She finally spoke. "I like that idea. We wouldn't have to do fancy."

"But I like you dressed up fancy and all. You are so beautiful, you don't get to do that enough."

"Redmond! We do a dress up dinner of some kind every week."

"I know." He kissed her again. "But I still like it when you dress up, just for me." He reached into his pocket, withdrawing a box, and opening it. "I had this made from some of the jewels I found. They were turned over to me as the authorities couldn't find the owners."

She stared at the delicate bracelet he held, tiny rubies sparkling from it, tears forming in her eyes. "Redmond? It's beautiful. But why rubies?"

"Proverbs 31, sweetheart. I have found a wife who is worth more to me and to God than all the rubies in the world. When you see the bracelet, I want you to remember that."

She turned, her arms around his neck as she sobbed briefly, before she sat back, her eyes on his even as she wiped away tears. "You're giving me jewels and praise. But what I have to give you? It's living." She pointed at the box he hadn't noticed before.

He reached for it, his hands stopping as the box moved, his eyes on her, seeing the mischief in her face. He opened it, and then with an exclamation pulled out a small border collie puppy.

"A puppy?"

She nodded. "Lad will stay with Dad. He's trained in search and rescue, which I can't do any more. This little girl will help heal our hearts."

"That she will." Redmond laughed as he put up a hand to fend off the tongue. "Does she have a name?"

Sloane shook her head. "She's yours. You have to name her."

"I do, do I?" He studied the pup, his heart full, thanksgiving raising to God for the happiness and freedom he found in Sloane. "Well, let's see. She needs a special name."

"She does." Sloane waited, a smile of contentment on her face.

"Laycee. That's it. Laycee."

Sloane's head rested against Redmond's shoulder as a hand reached out to touch the pup. "A good name for a little girl."

"I love you, Sloane. You make me complete." Redmond sat back, content, knowing that his family was safe, his siblings married and happy, and knowing that Sloane's brothers were content with the ladies they had found to share their lives with. God had blessed them, he thought,

and in ways they had not chosen to travel
but that He had taken them on.

Dear Readers

Thank you for choosing to read the story of Redmond Stuart and his lady, Sloane Everett, book five in His Stormchasers

Redmond, the oldest of the Stuart siblings, needed to wait until his siblings were settled with their life mates before he moved on with his life. I didn't expect him to go through what he and Sloane did, but I knew his story would be the culmination of the trials and mystery surrounding the Stuart family.

He and Sloane went through quite a storm, arriving safely through it. How many storms have you face or are facing in life? Be confident that you are not alone, never alone. God is always there, His hand on you, providing a refuge, a shelter in the storm. One of my favourite hymns as a child was one about finding shelter in a storm. God had provided that for me more often than I do. Trust Him, always.

God bless.

Ronna

www.ingramcontent.com/pod-product-compliance
Lightning Source LLC
Chambersburg PA
CBHW060858210726
48293CB00006B/1862